Love You Like A Love Song, Book 2

A Contemporary Romance
By Michele Callahan

Copyright 2016 Michele Callahan
All Rights Reserved

Copyright

Copyright 2016 Michele Callahan
Alone With You:
 Love You Like A Love Song, Book 2
Cover design Copyright 2016
by Michele Callahan
Photo Copyright vladthefool - Fotolia
Photo Copyright Studio10Artur – BigstockPhoto

Literary Work, First Edition. February 2016
 ISBN-13: 978-1530056644
 ISBN-10: 1530056640
Copyright 2016 by Michele Callahan
Published By Tydbyts Media
 All rights reserved.

This book is a work of fiction. Names, people, places and events are completely a product of the author's imagination or used fictitiously. Any resemblance to any persons, living or dead, is completely coincidental.

Alone With You
(Musical Arrangement and Song Lyrics)
Music and Lyrics: Copyright 2016 by
Michele Callahan and Lauren Kayley

Album Cover design Copyright 2016 by Michele Callahan and RomCon Custom Covers
Released by Michele Callahan/Tydbyts Media
 All rights reserved.

Acknowledgements

I owe a lot of people a sincere and heartfelt *thank you* for helping me pull this project together.

To my family, for putting up with my unfinished sentences, terrible cooking, and general weirdness. I am the luckiest woman in the world.

To Lauren (you'll all know her name someday) for taking my lyrics and turning them into such a beautiful melody. You helped make Jake and Claire's love story come to life. I can't play an instrument or sing a solid note to save my life, so their song would just be words on paper without you. You brought it to life and gave the song a voice.

To the awesome recording guru and guitar genius, JT Nolan, for his hours in the recording studio humoring a crazy romance author. Without your knowledge, skill, and amazing suggestions the song, Alone With You, would not exist.

To Mary Moran, editor extraordinaire. You rock! And you kick my ass. Both are talents for which I am extremely grateful.

To my Beta Readers, Review Team and friends for all your help and support. I love you guys.

To my writing buddies, who are always there when I need help, and who tackle the job of keeping me sane on this crazy journey: Vanessa Vale, S.E. Smith, Cynthia Woolf, Karen Docter, Maggie Mae Gallagher, and Cate Rowan. (Awesome authors and amazing women – you should check them out!)

And I bow my head with gratitude for the years I spent with CJ (Jan) Snyder. Amazing author. Even more incredible friend. You've been gone two years now, and I still miss you like it was yesterday. But I know, every time my fingers touch the keyboard…you're there. *Cheep-Cheep, baby*.

And finally, to YOU, dear reader. A book is just a string of words until those words are shared. Thank you for sharing this story with me.

Prologue

Jake Walker rang the doorbell and waited. A few seconds later, Mrs. Klasky opened the door in a pair of navy-blue pants and an oversized, cream-colored sweater. She had to be at least seventy years old, but she looked ten years younger.

"I'm so sorry about your mom, honey." She grabbed him by the arm and pulled him inside before closing it softly behind him. "You're the first one here."

"Figures." Jake took off his hat and held it down so he could tap the rim against the outside of his thigh. He was always the first one everywhere. His three brothers seemed to have a problem telling time. He followed her into the kitchen, past a wall filled with family photos and sepia-toned portraits of the Klasky family's ancestors, and sat down in his usual spot at the Klasky kitchen table in the hardwood oak chair closest to the twenty-year-old sofa covered with a paisley print and colors that he'd been told dated back to the 1970s.

"Here you go, dear." Mrs. Klasky set a glass of lemonade in front of him and he took a sip.

"Thanks." Fresh squeezed and real sugar, just like Mom used to make. His eyes actually misted and he looked up at the ceiling for a moment, waiting for the ache behind his eyes to pass. He'd cried enough. Boys lost their mothers every day. He was twenty-four, not twelve. He had to get his shit together and remember that some boys didn't have a mother at all.

The doorbell chimed and Mrs. Klasky excused herself for about a minute before leading two of his three brothers into the kitchen. Derek was the oldest, and the meanest, but Jake had leaned on that toughness more than once growing up. Derek ran a custom motorcycle shop in downtown Denver and looked the part—biker boots, black leather jacket and tattoos. Mitchell, on the other hand, was a second year surgical resident at the local trauma hospital. As much as Derek looked like a rebel, Mitchell looked like a city boy, with his hair too long for Jake's taste, expensive clothes and a sports car. Jake preferred his jeans, work boots, and truck. If he tried to wear the fancy crap his brother did, Jake knew he'd just look like a stray dog at a poodle party. Too big. Too rough. Too dirty.

After a couple of hard slaps on the back, the doorbell rang again.

"That'll be Chance." Mrs. Klasky disappeared again and came back with his brother Chance, the newly blooded attorney just a year out of law school.

"Chance." Derek got up from his seat at the end of the table and wrapped Chance up in a hug.

"Hey, loser." After a quick hug, Chance patted Derek on the shoulder. Jake and Mitchell took their turns. Normally, they weren't huggers, but being here today was making Jake's head trip, and he figured it was doing the same for his brothers.

"Late to the party, as usual." Jake

grabbed Chance and lifted him off the floor as if his brother were a little girl. Jake was the youngest, but all three of his older brothers were at least five inches and fifty pounds lighter. And as the baby, Jake never passed up an opportunity to rub their noses in the fact that he could kick every single one of their sissy-boy asses.

"And you still smell like cow patties and hay bales." Chance chuckled and Jake grinned back. His older brothers, Chance in particular, told Jake that he was the only one who was adopted. And Jake had spent several weeks believing their bullshit. He'd been five years old at the time. He'd cried to his mother, who'd told him the truth.

They were all adopted.

"Tough love, brother. But you smell like you had your ass wiped by a bathroom attendant with a perfumed moist towelette. You turning into one of those metrosexual, city boys?" Jake set him back down and Mitchell took his place, giving Chance a hard time. Mitchell was the only one who spent more time in the city than Chance did.

"Naw, man. That would be me."

Mitchell grinned and grabbed Chance around the shoulders. Mitchell lived in the city now, but ran for the mountains every chance he got. Hell, his brother texted them all pictures hanging from the side of a rock wall in a sleeping bag a couple hundred feet up the side of a cliff. Mitchell lived for the adrenaline rush of the emergency room. Gory gunshot wounds and stabbings made his brother happier than the steady stream of nurses he was always dating.

Chance stood there in his suit, and as usual, he was the only one in a tie. Even Mr. Klasky, his mother's eighty-year-old attorney, was in khakis and a golf shirt.

"Now that you're all here, we can begin." Mr. Klasky rolled in a small television with the old-fashioned VCR combo. Jake kicked out a chair and Chance sat down at the kitchen table, tugging on his tie.

They all thanked Mrs. Klasky respectfully as she served them lemonade and a tray of chocolate chip cookies, just as she'd been doing since they were in grade school.

When she settled against the wall,

Jake offered her his seat, but she shooed him away. "You boys are going to want to be sitting down for this."

"All due respect, Mr. Klasky, but Mother's estate was taken care of months ago when she first got sick." Chance was the lawman, so Jake was happy to let him speak legalese with Klasky.

"Yes. Yes. I know." The older man bent over, looking for an outlet in the wall so he could plug in the dinosaur of a television.

"Then why are we here?" Chance looked from Mr. Klasky, who had finally found an outlet and was shoving the electrical prongs into it, to his wife, who glowered at him with a raised eyebrow until he added, "Sir."

Satisfied, Mr. Klasky stood tall and rubbed his hands together like an excited schoolboy. "Well, boys, I promised your momma that I would get you all together today, six weeks to the day after she passed. God rest her soul."

"But why? Everything's been handled."

"Not everything." Mrs. Klasky pulled four envelopes from her apron pocket. Each looked like it would hold an oversized birthday card. She walked to the table and handed one to each of them. "Don't open them yet. You have to watch the video first."

Jake felt a lump in his throat as he traced the outline of his name written on the front of his card. He felt like they'd all been caught in some kind of evil time warp. His mother's distinct cursive handwriting on the outside of the card made him miss her more. She'd written his name in red ink on the white envelope. Red, because when he was nine years old, he'd told her that red was his favorite color. He looked up to check his brothers' cards. Sure enough, their mother had written each of their names on an envelope. Chance's card was green, and Jake smiled. Who could forget his brother's obsession with The Incredible Hulk? Mitchell's envelope was faded now, but red. And Derek? Mr. black leather and tattoos held an envelope that was a shockingly bright yellow.

"Holy hell." Jake leaned back in his seat and started tapping his cowboy hat against his knee.

Mr. Klasky shoved an old VHS tape into the player and the fuzzy screen went black for a few seconds. Jake heard the whirring of the tape as it played, and grinned. Mom always hated technology. It had taken him three years just to talk her into a cell phone. His grin faded as her voice echoed through the Klaskys' kitchen. And, oh boy, were they going to be in trouble. He knew that tone of voice, the devious quality that had kept her one step ahead of all four hardheaded teenage boys for so many years.

" Hello, my precious boys. I'm going to make this tape and give it to Mr. Klasky just in case something happens to me. I don't plan on going anywhere, but if I do, I want you boys to know I loved you more than anything and I was always proud, every single day, to be your mother."

Jake sniffed and turned his head away. No more waterworks. Christ.

"You boys know how much I always pushed you to follow your own hearts. Follow your dreams, I say. Well, I've been thinking about this a lot this past year. Derek is fourteen now, and I see it happening already.

"Life is going to get ahold of you boys,

and drain your dreams right out of you. I know. The real world is hard and unforgiving. Boys don't get to have dreams anymore. They have to be men. The world is going to expect you to be hard. And I know you can be hard as nails. All of you. I know where you came from. You were born into a hard world. I tried to show you a different life, but I'm afraid. I'm afraid you're going to grow up and forget who you really are. I don't want you to forget your dreams.

"So, I did something a little crazy. Maybe you'll remember, maybe you won't, but on my birthday this year, I asked each of you to write a very special card—"

Jake looked down at the card with dawning horror. Fuck no. He didn't even want to open it. He didn't want to relive that day, any more than he wanted to relive what happened eight years later.

Heartbreak. That was what he was holding in his hands.

His mother's laughter filled the quiet kitchen and the moment felt surreal. She was right there, on that little screen, smiling and happy and beautiful.

"I'm going to ask Mr. Klasky to hold on to these cards for a while. Someday, I'll

die. Maybe I'll be ninety, maybe not, but if I'm gone and you need reminding, he's going to remind you of who you really are."

She got serious and leaned forward until her face filled the entire screen.

"I love you. Each and every one. And you each made a promise to me, all those years ago. And dead or not, I expect you to keep it."

Then she laughed again. *"Dead or not. How's that for a good one? I love you. Don't forget who you were born to be. Open your cards now. Read them. And above all, remember why you wrote them. Keep your promises. I love you, and you know I'll be watching."*

Jake ignored his brothers, who all sat in stunned silence. God only knew what they'd written down in their cards, but he knew exactly what he'd written in his on that day in third grade. His mother had made him write down three things, but he was only worried about one of them. Number one on his list.

Claire Miller...

The only girl who ever truly broke his heart.

Chapter One

Six Months Later – Amazon River Basin, Brazil

Claire Miller wiped at the sweat on her brow with her forearm and continued to brush away the last bits of rock and debris that kept her from her prize. She'd found a new piece of pottery, likely at least five thousand years old, and she could feel the past calling to her through the layers of dirt and rubble, almost as if the ghosts of the ancient woman who had left the pottery in this cave was standing behind her, leaning over her shoulder, watching and waiting for Claire to touch what she had once touched, to feel what she had felt. Waiting to live again, through Claire.

The past was waiting to be brought into the present and she lived for that moment of discovery, the split second between nothing and something. Every artifact was like a piece of the past haunting the present, longing to be seen and felt, yearning to exist again, just for her.

She gently lifted the small pot from the earth and held it in the palm of her hand, marveling at the fact that it was in one piece. It was small and, to Claire's delight, the etched patterns were plainly visible. As she gently ran her fingertip along the edges of the piece, she could almost feel the hands that once held this pot, feel the strength that had forged the ancient stone and invested hours in making it beautiful. Sometimes, Claire swore she could actually feel the ancient people's joys and their struggles to survive. The people, who had been here in this cave, were real to her, and it was her sacred duty to protect their story and bring them back to life.

"We have to pack up soon, Claire." Emily was shoving gear into her backpack on Claire's left. Emily was a friend of hers from university, her roommate back home, and a fellow archeology graduate. They'd been lucky enough to travel the world together.

Claire loved every trip, every new location, new food, and new adventure. They'd been here for five weeks now and their time was about up. In less than a week, she'd be home.

All around her, the excavation team scrambled to put things away and pack up the day's artifacts for safe shipment to the museum where each piece would be inspected, cataloged and cleaned.

"I know. I know." Claire sat cross-legged on the ground and cradled the pot in the palm of her hand, unwilling to give it up just yet. "Isn't it beautiful?" She tilted her head to get a better look. "Some of the paint is still visible."

"It's a great piece, Claire. Get it labeled and pack it up. We have to get out of here. It's supposed to rain in about an hour." Howard Pierson, the team leader from the sponsor museum, shrugged his giant backpack onto his shoulders and wiped his face off with a handkerchief. Early June in Brazil meant eighty-degree days, high humidity, and only a few hours left until the afternoon rain made driving out on the trails a risky endeavor.

"Stinking rain." If she could, Claire

would just camp up here and keep digging all night. She could crawl back into the cave where Howard and a couple of the guys had a second pit going. She could dig by lamplight if she had to. Flashlight? If it weren't for the mosquitos and the snakes, she'd be tempted.

Claire crawled out of the digging pit on her hands and knees and scurried over to their supplies to carefully label and pack the artifact in the plain brown tackle box they'd converted to tool kits. When the pot was safely stowed, she pulled a water bottle from her backpack and drank half of it. It was hot and she felt like she was melting. They were a good quarter-mile hike up the mountain and they had to haul their gear out on their backs. Far below, two all-terrain vehicles waited to take them back to the small Brazilian town of Monte Alegre where their hotel and a soft bed waited. A few miles away, the big black mushroom-shaped Pedra Pintada rock rose like a friend waving to her in the distance. Twenty-five years ago, one of her archeology idols, Ann Roosevelt, had discovered the famous cavern holding artifacts and paintings dating back more than ten thousand years.

Roosevelt had rewritten history with that discovery, and Claire longed to make the same kind of epic announcement to the world one day. She wanted to be the one who buried her hands in the ground and found something that would change the way the world thought about itself. Claire wanted to leave her mark on history.

But not today. She shoved her water back into a side pocket on her pack. The sun rose early and set early here. By the time they drove the winding roads back to town it would be dark before they made it back to civilization, and she was tired.

Claire lifted her backpack and braced her feet apart to balance its weight. It wasn't light, and her back was already sticky and wet where her sweat had soaked through her t-shirt and shorts. She stank like dirt, sweat, valiant but ineffective antiperspirant, and insect repellant. "I smell like a chemical factory."

Emily laughed. She looked as gross as Claire felt. Emily's dark blonde hair looked three shades of brown and stuck to her face and head beneath her hat. Sweat ran down Emily's temples and soaked her shirt with the same v-shaped pattern above her cleavage and at the small of her back that Claire's filthy T-shirt displayed. They were both walking antiperspirant commercials. Not that it helped here, where the air was so sticky that the moment she dried off after a shower, she was wet again.

Emily lifted her arm and took a quick sniff of her armpit with a completely disgusted face. "We all stink. Freaking mosquitos."

"Better than donating blood, I guess. Or getting sick."

Claire had suffered the bite of multiple needles over the last few years while being vaccinated against everything from Typhoid and Yellow Fever, to Rabies. She figured she was a walking science experiment. Still, there were new diseases popping up all the time, and the freaking mosquitos always seemed to be in that equation somewhere.

"True." Emily lifted her pack and Claire fell into step behind her, as the whole crew marched down the hiking trail. There were nine members of the team, and she and Emily were the only women—which was typical. This trip, the guys were pretty decent. They weren't crude, disrespectful, or pushy, which was nice for a change. Their excavation team consisted of two older men from the museum who were friends with Howard, two others in their twenties who were both married that she and Emily knew from school, and their guide, *Senhor* Gomes, who was a local archeologist and their liaison with the Brazilian authorities. He was also fluent in both Portuguese and French. Claire spoke a bit of Spanish, but would have been lost down here without him.

The fact that every member of the team was married except Claire and Emily was also typical.

Seemed women were expected to let their husbands pursue their passions and roam the world having adventures.

Women were expected to settle down, get pregnant, and stay put.

Fuck that.

Every time she thought about it, she

got pissed off and sad at everything she'd left behind...or more accurately, who. But she shoved that shit down and kept hiking. Jake Walker was past history. That ship sailed an eon ago. Her biggest problem was that she'd never really gotten over him. He was too freaking perfect in every way but one.

He wanted a housewife, a little woman to share the ranch life with him and raise horses. And he was a great, amazing, sexy-as-hell cowboy who could probably have just about any women he wanted in his bed. His babies would look like cherubic little blond versions of himself, too cute to handle with shy smiles, big eyes and chubby little arms that couldn't wait to hug everyone. His kids would be perfect in every way. It was a dream life for just about any woman. Well, any woman but her.

Shaking off thoughts of the past, Claire took a deep breath and admired the view. The Amazon River Basin stretched out below them like a picture from a postcard. The area was rich with biodiversity. Everywhere she looked things were green, and growing, and filled with life. The birds were colorful and wild, and the flowers and trees were so different from the dry sagebrush and pine trees of her home in Colorado that she felt like she was in another world.

The team was about halfway down the mountain when her satellite phone rang.

No one called her when she was on a dig, unless it was bad news. She would video chat with her friends and family from the hotel when she had internet access, but the phone was for emergencies only. Only three people had her number: Her parents, Emily, and her boss back in California.

Emily stopped in front of her and Claire swung around so her friend could dig the phone out of the side pocket of her pack.

"You want us to wait?" Howard half shouted over his shoulder from the head of the line.

"No. Go ahead. We'll be right behind you." Emily answered for her and Claire smiled over her shoulder at her friend in gratitude. She had no idea if it was her parents or her boss. Either way, she didn't need seven sets of male ears listening to every word. Claire held her hand out to the side and Emily placed the ringing phone in her palm from behind so Claire could answer the call.

"Hello?"

"Claire, honey? Is that you?"

"Mom? Is everything okay?"

"Where are you, Claire? Do you have a minute? I can call back later." Her mother's voice wavered and Claire's stomach dropped like a two-ton brick. Something was wrong.

"Mom. I'm fine. I'm still in Brazil but we're heading home in a few days. What's wrong?"

"Honey, it's your dad. Widowmaker threw him and they're taking him in to do a brain scan right now. He's hurt pretty bad."

A million scenarios rushed through her mind, everything from a broken neck to shattered bones, and she felt an odd calm settle inside her mind. Claire turned her back to the steep rock that ran along one side of the trail and leaned her pack against it for extra support. Every horseman knew that he could be thrown on any given day. The risk came with the thrill of riding, but her dad had been riding that stubborn stallion for years. The horse was ornery, but not mean or unpredictable. "What happened? How bad is it?"

Emily peered up into Claire's face with a worried frown and wide green eyes, and Claire whispered, "It's my dad. He got thrown off his horse."

"Oh, no." Emily paled, her normally cheery face stoic as Claire waited silently for her mom to continue.

"They think he's going to be all right, but he's got a concussion, broken ribs and he separated his shoulder. They're going to put some screws in his collarbone to reattach it." Her mom sounded fairly calm, considering.

"How bad is the concussion?"

"They don't know yet, dear. He went for his scans but we don't have the results yet. You know how that goes. And now they're talking about surgery. But they said they want to wait to make sure his brain's okay before they put him under general anesthesia, which means we're going to be here for a few days. And he's in a lot of pain."

Claire's mind was clear, but her pulse was pounding. Her dad was like a rock. Her rock. He couldn't' be hurt or in the hospital. He could not have a brain injury. That reality simply did not make sense in her world.

"Do you need me to come home?"

Her mom started crying, and that was the only answer Claire needed.

"I'll catch a plane tomorrow, Mom." Hopefully, she could catch a plane at the local airport in Monte Alegre. If not, she'd have to take the bus to the Santarem airport, which was almost sixty miles away, but still doable. "I'll be home as soon as I can. If I get lucky, I'll be there tomorrow night."

"I'm so sorry, sweetheart. I don't want to mess up your trip."

"You aren't messing up anything. I'm already on my way."

Claire talked to her mom for another couple minutes and ended the call. She tapped the phone against her thigh and exhaled with a huff. "Shit."

"That didn't sound good. How's your dad?"

"He's got a brain injury and he needs surgery on his shoulder. He's going to be in the hospital for a few days at least, and my mom needs help." Claire looked out over the trees and swallowed back a lump in her throat.

"You okay? We gotta move. They're already loading gear." Emily tilted her head to the side to indicate the vehicles parked below them. Claire glanced over the side of the cliff to see the men loading their packs, a couple already lounging around waiting for them.

"I'm fine. Let's go."

Emily nodded and took off at a quick pace. Claire was right on her heels, but she felt like a huge liar. She wasn't okay. She was going home for the first time in seven years. She'd seen her parents two or three times a year since she'd left Colorado. They came out to California regularly to visit, but Claire never went home.

Too many memories waited for her there. She loved the past, as long as it wasn't her own.

Chapter Two

Two days later, Claire Miller pulled into the long driveway that led to the Walker family ranch and sighed. She was home, back in Colorado on her old stomping grounds, and it hurt just as much as she thought it would.

Seven years evaporated like they'd never existed. Everything at the ranch looked exactly the way it had the day she'd left town, but she knew one major difference waited...Jake's mom was gone.

That loss hit her harder now. For the first time in her life, Mrs. Walker wouldn't be on the front porch smiling and waving, or bringing her and Jake a pitcher of lemonade in the barn. She wouldn't be in the kitchen making fried chicken or harassing her four boys about their homework or their girlfriends, and generally in that order.

Claire half expected the place to look as sad on the outside as she suddenly felt on the inside, but the world never stopped spinning, no matter who was lost. The large red barn was freshly painted, the outbuildings were overflowing with riding tack, hay, and tractors. The riding and roping arenas were often used and the horses' hooves made sure nothing could survive inside the ring, not even a single blade of grass. And that big yellow ranch house, where she'd spent the happiest days of her life? Bright spring flowerpots hung from hooks on the porch ceiling and were filled to overflowing with a mix of brightly colored flowers. The porch swing was bright yellow, green, and white, with pillows precisely placed and ready for her to curl up and take a nap. The railings were bright white and clean, and the front door was a deep hunter green with a sunflower door knocker and matching welcome mat¬¬—just the way Mrs. Walker had always liked it. Jake's mom once said that a place should feel like home before you even open the door, and Claire fought back burning tears as she realized she hadn't felt this sense of arriving at a familiar place for a very long time.

She drove past the house toward the barn. Pine trees lined the drive and property, ponderosa, lodgepole, and blue spruce trees were scattered like God had been driving seventy down Highway 7 and thrown seeds out the window of his pickup. Quivering aspen trees popped up in spaces between, while tall grass and random growths of aster, daisies, columbine, and other wildflowers were scattered on the ground and in the ditches. Unlike Brazil, the Colorado heat was bone dry, like holding one's hand above the burner on a stovetop. Waves of warmth turned the grass brown where the snow had long ago melted and the rocky ground was dry as a desert.

It still looked like home. Smelled like home, with horses, hay, pine trees, and dust filling the truck's cab despite the air-conditioning system's filters. Still felt like home, too...and all because *he* was here, somewhere. She could feel Jake Walker in her blood, her entire body buzzed with the possibility of seeing him again.

Jake.

Just thinking about him made her chest ache. Apparently, her heart hadn't forgotten a damn thing either. She had hoped the years would have dulled the pain, but no such luck. Just seeing that house, and the white porch swing where they'd spent so many hours together, stabbed through her heart like a knife.

"Get it together, woman. It's been over for a long time."

Over and done. Finished. Seven years had come and gone, and she was still in love with him. She had her reasons for leaving him and nothing had changed. Nothing. Hell, the way she'd left things that hot summer night—Jake probably hated her. And she hoped he did. It would make being back in town a lot easier.

The half-mile road used to be dirt, back when she'd walked it every day on her way to see her best friend, Jake Walker. The same old gnarled cottonwood thrust up out of the ground in the middle of Jake's backyard, like a lone wolf howling at the bright sunny sky. Pasture and meadow grass stretched out on both sides of the drive to the barn. Perfectly even white fences sectioned the Walkers' thousand-acre ranch into large areas, and everywhere she looked horses of every size and color roamed.

The Walker Ranch was well known throughout the country for its excellent breeding stock and training programs. Mrs. Walker had been a big part of that. The locals had considered her their own special version of a horse whisperer, and her son, Jake, was rumored to have the same magical touch.

Claire didn't doubt that for a second. She'd always thought his touch was magical, too.

She checked her side mirrors and drove slowly so as not to disturb the mare and stallion she had loaded onto the horse trailer she was towing. Her dad wasn't going to be able to take care of them for a couple months and her mom just didn't need the stress. The doctors told her dad he shouldn't get back in the saddle for at least three months, which was too long to let the horses go without proper exercise. And there was no way her tiny mother was hauling hay.

So here she was, bright and early on Thursday morning, delivering horses to the Walker ranch. Jake was going to board the horses for her dad for three months, for free.

Of course Jake would do that...take care of her parents. She should be happy, but it just made her angry. Why couldn't the man be an asshole? That would make her life so much easier. Loving him sucked. Thank God she'd be gone soon.

Three weeks was all the time she could get off from work. She was supposed to be in Brazil for another week working with the team to catalog and ship their artifacts to the museum in California. Emily was covering for her on that end. After that, she was a free agent. Her Master's Thesis was in final review and she already had a couple of good job offers on the table from reputable programs, as well as two museums. As soon as she got that stupid piece of paper, she'd be done with school. Finished with grad school and trying to figure out where she wanted to go next...Egypt or back to

Mexico on an Aztec dig.

Either would be fabulous. Both, even better.

But that was a problem for another day. Today, she was here on the Walker Ranch, and she felt like she was stepping into a minefield.

Thankfully, she wouldn't have to see Jake. She hoped that she wouldn't see him at all. He had a full staff working the ranch and her appointment was with a woman named Mindy, who was in charge of Jake's boarding stables.

Her dad's large black truck bumped and rolled on its way up to the main stable, the place that Mindy had told her to drop off the horses when she'd spoken to her a short while ago on the phone.

Claire drove around the circular area in front of the large barn until she had the horse trailer lined up with the gates. She didn't expect trouble from the mare, but Widowmaker, the black-and-white tobiano stallion, was three-quarters American Saddlebred and had the temperament to match. That horse could be a real pain in the ass if he wasn't in a good mood. And, since her dad hadn't taken him out riding since the accident, the stubborn horse was definitely not in the best of spirits.

She could totally relate.

She shut down the chugging of the diesel engine and climbed down out of the truck's oversized cab. She jumped to the dirt with a quiet thump of an old pair of boots she'd dug out of the back of her closet and took a few seconds to straighten out her clothing and toss the tail of her long brown braid back over her shoulder. She was dirty, exhausted from almost thirty hours of travel with very little sleep, and bruised from loading the horses on her own. Mom and Dad were at the hospital doing the whole shoulder surgery thing today and she couldn't complain much. Since her dad's head injury hadn't been severe, she'd been determined to tackle the job herself.

As she walked toward the barn, the horses greeted her through the trailer's long, rectangular slits and Claire could hear their big hooved feet shifting impatiently inside. Everything about this place was so familiar, the smell of dust and hay, the quiet whinnies of other horses curious about the new arrivals, and the picture-perfect angle of the sun's rays. She glanced up at the house and saw that her favorite sitting spot on Jake's back porch looked as welcoming as ever, perfectly shaded and lined with blooming flower boxes. Big country house. Big wraparound porch. It was beautiful, and too perfect to be real.

A bittersweet pain speared the back of her eyeballs and she knew if she didn't start moving, she'd cry. That was one reason she didn't come back to town. Most days, she was fine. But when she stopped moving, or when things got too quiet, she missed home. She missed him. And when she'd heard that Jake's mom had passed, she'd nearly broken down and called.

"Hello there! You must be..."

"Claire?"

The woman's voice came from the direction of the barn and Claire looked over to see an older woman, near fifty, walking toward her. The other voice, the one she would probably respond to, even if she was unconscious and in a coma, she knew all too well.

Claire plastered a smile on her face and turned to face them. "You must be Mindy."

"Pleased to meet you." Mindy was average size, with a lined face, kind blue eyes, and work-roughened hands. Claire liked her instantly. She knew a horsewoman when she saw one.

"Me, too." Claire shook her hand with a warm smile and delayed the inevitable as long as possible.

A half step behind Mindy stood Jake. Shit. He looked even better than she remembered. His broad shoulders and chest had been built tossing hay bales, and he'd matured, filled out even more since she's seen him last. What had been impressive in a seventeen-year-old boy was devastating to her senses now that he had grown into a man. Still tall, so tall that he made her feel small and feminine, even though she was just a couple inches shy of six foot herself.

"Hi, Jake."

"Claire. I didn't know you were in town."

"I'm only here for a few weeks to help out after my dad has surgery."

"Of course." Jake said it like he wasn't surprised that she wasn't sticking around. It was true, but his blasé attitude still rankled. He glanced from the trailer back to her. "You bring your dad's horses?"

Claire shoved her hands into the front pockets of her jeans. "Yeah. Widowmaker and Starlight." Starlight was her mare, the horse she'd spent hours riding in high school—usually with Jake. Her mother rode the gentle mare these days, while her dad fed his wild side working with the troublemaker...and getting his stalwart old body tossed like a rag doll's into the dirt.

Jake looked her over, from the dusty toes of her hiking boots to the wild bits of hair that had escaped her French braid. She looked a mess and she knew it. When she was about to run for cover, he turned his attention to the horses and walked up to greet them through the openings in side of the beat-up white trailer.

"Hey there, boy. I bet you're ready to get out of there." Jake pulled a treat of some kind from the front pocket of his jeans and Widowmaker whinnied and talked back, as if Jake could speak horse. Hell, maybe he could. Jake walked back to her and held out his hand to take Widowmaker's lead rope from her. She handed it over as Mindy pulled the pin and swung open the back of the slant-load trailer.

Claire stepped back and let Jake take over unloading the stallion with Mindy's help. Eager to be out of the trailer, Widowmaker walked out with Jake a hell of a lot faster than he'd gone in. Typical. Claire tried to ignore the scene as Jake and Mindy both patted and soothed the horse once they had him on the ground. A handful of treats, and the stallion followed Mindy to the pasture like a docile pony.

If only all men were so easily tamed.

Claire sighed and hopped up into the trailer with Starlight's bright red lead rope in hand. She ducked under the center gate and clipped her mare onto the lead. Jake hopped up behind her to help and she nodded to him to indicate she was ready for him to open the middle gate.

So easy, slipping back into her old

rhythm with him. She still knew every move he was going to make before he made it, every step and every look, and every motion of those big, strong hands.

She even knew he was going to take Starlight's lead from her before he did it. What she didn't anticipate was the flare of anger his take-charge attitude inspired. That ire lent some steel to her spine and she squashed her longing for him like a spider under a boot heel. She'd left for a reason. She needed to remember that. Nothing had changed. "I've got her. Thanks."

"I can lead her out."

"I said, I've got her." Claire refused to look him in the eye and didn't bother asking herself where all this irrational fire was coming from. She knew exactly why she was about to lose her mind, and it was the reason she had avoided coming to the ranch all these years. Seeing Jake again, now, made the raw edges of her life bleed all over again. It was like she'd never left.

"All right. Don't get your panties in a bunch."

"What?" He did *not* just say that.

"Nothing." Jake turned away and

walked back up into the trailer to secure the center gate, then hopped out, closed the gate, latched and pinned it for her drive home. Such a gentleman, which made her feel like screaming on the inside.

She tugged on Starlight's lead and the horse followed her in the direction Mindy had taken the stallion. The dirt trail had been worn into the ground by tractor and truck tires, and led to a pasture about a quarter mile from the main house.

Starlight nudged her in the side of the head and Claire absently reached over to pat her old friend on the nose. Jake hadn't been the only thing she'd missed. She and Starlight had been best friends since she was thirteen. The mare had arrived at her dad's small farm with a bright white bow tied around her neck on Claire's birthday. In the horse-breeding world, Starlight was worthless, the unplanned foal of an old quarter horse sire and an American Saddlebred dam.

Her dad had laughed and said that Starlight's mother had gone slumming. Claire didn't care where the horse had come from, only that Starlight was a beautiful chestnut with white feet and a white star on her forehead, and she loved to run. Her parents' small property backed to national forest lands which she'd explored for hours, covered hundreds of miles. With Jake. Always, things came back to Jake.

Claire rubbed Starlight's nose and picked up the pace. All she had to do was avoid Jake and get out of town as quickly as possible. That was the only way she could keep her head on straight. Her heart was a lost cause, and had been for years. But real love and real life didn't mix, at least not for her. Her job was her life now and that was just the way things worked out.

Claire chanced a glance back over her shoulder to see Jake leaning up against the split rail fence, arms crossed over that massive chest, and his hat back on his head, watching her walk away. This time, there was no confusion or hurt in his eyes. Those blue eyes of his were cold and hard. Unforgiving.

Well, tough shit. She'd done what she thought was best. And she'd do it again, because some things never changed. And Jake Walker was one of them.

Starlight whinnied and shoved into her hand. Claire sighed and turned back around.

Love was such a bitch.

Chapter Three

Jake had a prime spot for viewing Claire's curvy ass as she led Starlight to the south pasture. When Mr. Miller had called asking about boarding the two horses, Jake had refused to take the older man's money. They'd been family friends for as long as he could remember. Hell, his mom and Claire's had been best friends since the fifth grade.

And Claire? First day of school in the third grade, that was the moment he'd first set eyes on Claire Miller. She'd walked into class with that wild mane of dark brown hair, pink cowgirl boots, and a Texan accent, and he'd been a goner. The accent hadn't lasted much more than a year. The pink boots, a bit longer. But none of it mattered to him. Love at first sight. Lightning strike.

Name the fucking cliché, he'd felt it.

He'd gone home that night and announced to his mother that he was going to marry Claire Miller and have ten kids and live on the ranch forever.

His mom was already excited that her childhood friend had finally moved back home to Colorado with her husband. Mr. Miller spent the first half of his adult life chasing oil as a geologist for a huge petroleum company and the second half chasing chickens and cows. And Claire? She'd moved more often than an army brat before settling here. She made friends with ease but, for some unknown, unfathomable reason, she'd chosen him. Stuck out here in the middle of nowhere, his two older brothers, Derek and Mitchell, were too busy with their high school drama to pay attention to him. Chance was around, but he'd spent almost as much time with Claire as Jake had, at least until Chance got his driver's license. After that, his brother found every possible excuse to spend time in town.

There hadn't been a lot of other people around. He and Claire had been best friends because there really wasn't ever anyone else their age around. He was glad there hadn't been a bunch of girls around for her to giggle and play dress up with. She'd hung out with him, riding and exploring and talking about the world. And because he'd been totally, completely, head-over-heels in love with her, that had been enough.

And the idea of him and Claire getting married? Jake's mom had danced around the kitchen that night as he'd talked about how perfect he and Claire were for each other. For the next eight years, it had been perfect. Until he'd made his fatal mistake and forced his way out of the friend zone their senior year.

Claire had been all his for three amazing weeks. He'd been on top of the world, convinced that all of his dreams about Claire were about to come true. He'd even taken his mom into town and bought a diamond engagement ring with the money he'd saved from working three summers on the ranch and selling two of his best foals. Marriage. Kids. Forever. He'd wanted it all. But before he'd worked up the nerve to ask her to marry him, she told him that she was leaving and that she couldn't live on the ranch forever. She'd told him that he couldn't make her happy, hopped on an airplane to California, and he hadn't seen her since.

"Guess some things just don't work out, Mom." Jake knew he was talking to a ghost, but if his mom had ever planned on haunting her children, he knew this moment was one his mother wouldn't miss. Hell, if his mom's ghost were here, she'd be shoving him in Claire's direction and telling him to go talk to her.

Well, he didn't need his mother here to tell him what she would have wanted. He'd known Mom better than any of his brothers. He'd been the only one still at home when she'd gotten sick. He'd driven her to her chemo treatments and sat by her bed, reading to her and holding her hand when she was too sick to talk. He'd been the one watching her fade away, watching her refuse to eat, watching her turn gray and weak and sad.

Even thinking about those months was like a knife twisting in his gut, but he'd done it because he loved her.

Because she needed help and he'd helped her. He didn't resent his brothers for not being around as much. They'd done what they could, but they had school and jobs and businesses to run. He only had his mom and this ranch. Now, with Chance fuck only knew where in the world on any given day and his mom gone, some days it felt like all he had left were memories of what it meant to be family.

He'd lost his first family, and been lucky enough to find a second.

Now he'd lost that one, too.

And Claire was part of his family, whether she wanted to be or not. Hell, whether he wanted her to be or not. Seeing her again made places ache inside him that he'd all but forgotten he had. Deep, dark, dangerous places where he didn't want to be nice, didn't want to be a gentleman. Hell, when it came to Claire, he didn't want to hurt anymore. He just *wanted*. Period.

Claire. Here.

Fuck.

Jake watched her walk back from the pasture with a mixture of hurt and self-disgust at war in his chest. When he'd first seen her get out of that truck, his stubborn heart had raced in excitement, until his rational mind took over. She looked better than ever. Her fresh-faced youth had been replaced by a delicate maturity in the fine lines of her cheeks and full lips. He'd loved a girl all those years ago. Claire was all woman now, her features more refined, her brown eyes were darker and lacking the easy laughter he'd loved so much when he was a boy, and her body had filled out and curved in all the right places.

She didn't want you, asshole. Move on.

Claire had made her choice. She'd left him behind and finished school. Last he heard, she was working for some archeological program at a university in California and spending time at digs all over the world.

Claire Miller, world traveler. Adventurer. She was never coming back to him, to ranch life and midnight rides and skinny-dipping in the freezing-cold lake. He knew that for fact. But he was also part idiot, because he still had that fucking diamond ring in a drawer in his bedroom. No matter how many times he'd told himself to take it back, trade it in, or give it away, he'd never been able to let it go because it was hers.

He remained silent as she closed the distance between them and, for a moment, he thought she was going to walk right by him, get in her father's truck and drive away without saying a word. He wasn't sure if that would make him happy or just plain mad.

When she got within a few steps, she stopped and kicked at the dirt with her boots. "Thanks, Jake. For taking care of the horses for my dad."

"It's no big deal." And it wasn't. Not to him. It was what friends did. Neighbor helping neighbor. He had no idea where he'd gotten such old-fashioned ideas, maybe watching old *Ponderosa* reruns on cable, but he had them. All three of his brothers had gotten off the ranch and out of the country life as fast as they could. They all lived in Denver now, more than willing to leave their mother's ranch in his hands. And he was glad. He drove into the city once a month to have a beer with his brothers, and every time he hit that fucking I-25 traffic, he remembered why he hated city life.

"It is a big deal, Jake. At least to us. So, thank you." As if that were as long as she could stand to talk to him, she took off, heading toward her truck.

"Hold up, Claire. I need you to fill out some paperwork." He stood and closed the distance between them. She waited, arms crossed, for him to catch up.

"Okay. What paperwork?"

"A release for emergency vet treatment and a description of any special instructions or care the horses might need while they're here. Their previous training schedule, temperament, stuff like that."

"But don't you know all that stuff?"

"I do. But my staff doesn't."

"Oh." She sounded disappointed, maybe even annoyed at the prospect of filling out his standard paperwork. Either the horses were too much trouble, or she just didn't want to be around *him*.

Too bad. He'd planned on letting Mindy take care of the paperwork, but decided that if it bothered Claire to be around him, he'd enjoy making her suffer for a few more minutes.

She followed him into the house and he paused at her gasp.

"What?"

Claire walked over to his mother's favorite writing desk, an antique oak half table painted with delicate vines and pink roses. She ran her fingers over the smooth surface as she looked around. "The house looks exactly the same."

"Yeah, I guess it does." Jake looked around and tried to imagine the place through her eyes. He realized it was true...nothing had changed. "Mom wasn't big on change."

Claire smiled and the dimple in her left cheek teased him with a thousand memories of happier days. "True. I remember it took all four of you to convince her to get a cell phone." The Christmas before Claire left him, he'd banded together with his older brothers and bought their mom a brand new iPhone, paid in full with a year of service. Jake had spent several hours with her the next day trying to teach her how to use it.

"She never did like to text."

"Your mom was quirky, Jake, and

tough. I always loved that about her." Claire's smile evolved into a quiet laugh and Jake's gut clenched at the sound, so soft and sexy. But the smile faded and she turned to him with big, sad eyes. "I'm sorry you lost her. She was an amazing woman."

"Yeah, she was." His mom had adopted him when he was four. His three older brothers she'd adopted the year before, all from broken homes with fucked-up backgrounds. She'd kissed their bruises and kicked their asses until they all realized she wasn't going to let them win, and she wasn't going to go anywhere. After a couple of rough years, their family had gelled into a tightly knit unit. His brothers had his back, no matter what. And his mother had poured part of that fierce determination to build a family into this house, and into him. He'd felt lost since she died, off kilter, like his foundation was gone. Instead of feeling rock steady and as stable as the land under his feet, like he normally did, he felt like he was in a blowup raft drifting across the Atlantic. Alive, but scared shitless, with no land in sight.

All of which made him feel like a pussy. He couldn't talk to any of his brothers about it. They'd kick his ass and tell him to grow up. So he just suffered alone. He'd get over it eventually, but keeping the house the way his mom had always kept it helped him hold on to her. It made him feel like she was less gone. Sad. Pathetic. And one hundred percent true.

The same brown sofas filled the living room, sofas that he'd napped on, cried on, and spent days on while watching cartoons when he was sick with the flu. The same hand-knit afghans were draped over the couch backs, knitted by his mother—she'd made one for each of the boys on their thirteenth birthday. An old-fashioned cherry rocker rested in the corner near a matched pair of floor-to-ceiling bookshelves. That was his favorite chair, the place he'd spent many happy hours on his mother's lap when he was small and she would read stories to him.

His mother's odd collection of antique china filled a hutch in the dining room and the hardwood floors were covered by a large assortment of colorful rugs. The house looked exactly the same as it had for as long as he could remember. His mom had been gone for about a year, but he had no interest in changing anything. It felt familiar. When he walked in the door, it felt like home.

"So, where's this paperwork? The office?" Claire took off down the main hallway toward the back office and Jake hurried to keep up with her. She knew the layout of the house almost as well as he did. She'd spent half her childhood here.

"Just have a seat and I'll get it." He followed her into the office, which had been his domain for the last year. Before she'd gotten sick, his mom had taken care of the accounting and kept up with all the records. But over the last couple of years, Jake had gradually taken over, and the space reflected that. Gone were the potted plants and candles. The office looked like a working man's domain, with mud on the floor, tack on the seats, and muddy boots next to his chair where he'd kicked them off the night before. Stacks of horse training manuals, invoices, employee schedules, and feed order forms littered the desk, right next to the oversized computer monitor.

Jake sat down behind his desk. Claire sat in the short leather chair across from him and he pulled a fresh pile of paperwork from the two-drawer filing cabinet under the window. "The first page is a release for emergency veterinary care. The rest of it is feeding instructions, medication and training questions."

"Okay." Clair took the paperwork from him and reached up to tuck a strand of dark brown hair behind her ear as she read through the first page. "Do you have a pen?"

Jake felt the urge to face-palm, but restrained himself and gave her a pen from his center desk drawer. A small frown marred her brow as she focused on the paperwork, and he tried not to stare. He really did, but something about Claire Miller had always captured his attention. Always.

When she was eight and she'd walked into Mrs. Burnett's third grade classroom, it had been the way Claire had glided into the room like a princess, with her long brown hair flowing around her like the girls he'd seen in music videos. Then she'd sat down across from him and smiled.

Game over. He knew, right then and there, that he was going to marry her. Nine years old, and he had his life all planned out.

Unfortunately, Claire had other ideas. And sitting here, in the same room, with her sunshine-and-oranges scent drifting to him across the giant oak desk, that nine-year-old version of himself was shouting in triumph. *She's back!* In the deepest part of himself, he couldn't stop that little bastard from celebrating, and leaping around inside his rib cage like a bouncy ball.

But he hadn't been that naïve little boy in a long time. Not since Claire had looked him in the eye and broken his heart.

His heart and his mind were in an all-out civil war for control of his body, and they were tearing him in two as he watched her smooth white teeth lock onto her full bottom lip in concentration. She was more beautiful than ever. Her thick brown hair fell to her shoulder blades in the tail of an elaborate braid.

Her face was bare of makeup, but her pale skin looked smooth and refined. And her eyes, those coffee-colored eyes, were framed by lashes so thick he used to enjoy tickling his lips with them.

He adjusted in his chair to fight off the rising interest of his dick. Not cool. He'd only ever had a few nights with her, but the little fucker in his pants wanted more. Every cell in his body wanted more. Fuck, he still loved her. Probably always would. Which made this entire situation suck on so many levels he couldn't even begin to count them all.

His phone buzzed in his back pocket and he checked it quickly to make sure it wasn't anything urgent. When he saw the group text from his brothers confirming their boys' night out tomorrow, he replied to let them know he'd be there and shoved the phone back into his pocket. His brother, Chance, was getting married in six months to the love of his life. Chance was back in town for a lawyer friend's wedding this weekend and tomorrow night's monthly boy's night out was doubling as the bachelor party.

Normally, Jake looked forward to seeing his brothers, but hanging out and drinking with a room full of drunk idiots he didn't know was not his idea of a good time. He'd go anyway, because the truth was he missed Chance since his brother had fallen in love and left Denver in the rear view. Chance's fiancée, Erin, was a musician currently on tour with her new record label and Chance was along for the ride.

Yesterday, Jake had been looking forward to giving his brother hell. Now, staring down his own woman problems, he wasn't in the mood to tease any of his brothers about the opposite sex. Not when he was sitting here, getting his ass kicked by lust for a woman who'd dumped him cold a long, long fucking time ago.

"I think that's it." Claire signed the last page and glanced up at him.

"Okay." Jake reached across the desk and took the paperwork from her, giving it a thorough inspection. When it came to women, he was a fucktard. But when it came to horses, he didn't mess around and didn't take any chances. "What about riding? You want to come out and exercise Starlight, or do you want one of my guys to do it?"

"I haven't ridden a horse in a long time." Claire frowned and her shoulders drooped as she turned to stare out the window. For the first time he noticed the tired lines around her mouth and the dark circles under her eyes. He wanted to pull her into his arms and hold her, but he didn't dare move. She looked like she'd been through hell, and with her dad in the hospital he could totally relate.

"Then we need to change that." Jake lifted the stack of white paper and tapped it into a neat pile using the hard desk. "You love to ride, Claire. You always loved to ride."

She turned back to face him and he swore he saw the telltale glimmer of unshed tears begin to pool in her eyes. But as soon as he put the papers down and leaned closer, the shine was gone.

"You're right. I'll come out and ride her myself."

"Excellent." Not only would he not need to rearrange his staff schedules, he'd get to see Claire almost every day. Not that he cared. It was for Starlight's sake. The horse loved Claire almost as much as he did. "You said you're only in town for a few weeks?"

"Three weeks."

"Okay." Three weeks of internal civil war. Every time he saw her, his heart and his head would battle. Which would be fine. He could handle that, as long as his dick stayed out of it. "That should give me enough time to rearrange the other horses' exercise schedules."

Unable to sit, and stare, and *want* for another minute, Jake got to his feet and headed for the door. He almost made it. Almost. But she stood now, reached out with her hand and wrapped it around his forearm as he passed.

One touch, and his body jerked to a stop in reaction, not because he wanted to throw off that burning touch, but because he wanted to revel in the heat of her hand on his arm. It felt like a branding iron. He was still hers. He would always be hers. This weakness, this need for her, was going to ruin his life. He'd tried to move on, he really had. He'd even sucked it up and gotten engaged in college to a girl he hoped could make him happy. No such luck. She'd seen right through him and moved on. His obsession with Claire had already cost him a broken engagement and years of loneliness. After his fiancée, Courtney, left him, he'd tried meeting new people. His asshole brother, Mitchell, had posted a shirtless photo of Jake working with one of the horses and created an online dating profile without Jake's permission. Jake had played along and tried the online dating thing. He'd slept with other women over the years. But in the end, none of them had ever measured up to Claire.

His life would be so much easier if he didn't understand Claire's reasons for leaving, if he could just hate her fucking guts.

"Thank you, Jake. Thank you so much for helping us out like this."

"No problem." He looked down at her hand where it rested on his arm because he needed her to remove it. Shaking off her touch just wasn't an option for him. She would have to be the one to break contact. He was that much of a fucking masochist.

Instead of freeing him, she did something worse. She leaned up and pressed those petal-soft lips to his cheek. Less than a second of contact, and he had to bite his tongue to keep the rage and the pain from withering his body into a dead husk. This agony was his life now. This longing and regret that things would never be different. That he couldn't be what she needed him to be.

But he was a man now, with seven years of hell behind him. Claire was his kryptonite. He knew it, even if she didn't, which meant he'd have to do whatever he could to keep her at arm's length. She was leaving in three weeks, and who knew how long she'd be gone this time? A year? Ten?

He could hurt, and lust, and control himself for twenty-one days. But he couldn't let her back in. He couldn't touch her, or talk to her, or kiss her. Ever. Not if he wanted to have any hope of surviving the rest of his life without turning into a bitter, angry old man. Hell, he was still bleeding from their last encounter, and she'd been a lanky, seventeen-year-old girl.

Claire was tall, and curved like a

fantasy goddess come to life. And just as dangerous.

With a soft sigh she leaned back and broke all contact. A moment later she was gone, but Jake remained rooted to the spot until he heard the loud chug of her truck's diesel engine drive away. When the sound faded, he walked back behind his desk and removed the plain white envelope from the top drawer.

His hands shook as he opened the flap and pulled the card free. On the outside of the card was a comedic picture of a chestnut horse wearing sunglasses and a party hat. But it wasn't the outside that concerned him. He opened the card and read the very first of the three items on his list for the hundredth, hell, the thousandth time. He halfheartedly hoped for a miracle, for a blessing of divine intervention that would change what he'd written.

No such luck. Same ink. Same words. And the same thing still number one on the list, written in all capital letters in bright red ink.

Marry Claire Miller

Chapter Four

Claire drove home, ditched the horse trailer and headed into the city. She was supposed to meet her mom for lunch at the hospital. Per her mother's texts, the surgery was going well and everything was under control. The good news helped Claire relax a fraction, but not enough. Forty-five minutes later, when she pulled into the hospital parking lot, she still hadn't stopped shaking. Staring out the windshield, she had to work really hard to pay attention where she was driving. Her mind kept drifting back to Jake and his leather-and-pine cologne, those honest blue eyes, and those massive shoulders. The longer she sat still, the more she remembered.

She had to get out of this truck. Walk. Move. Distract herself.

Parking the truck on the outer edges

of the lot where there weren't any other cars, she shut down the engine and rested her forehead against her hands on the steering wheel.

Seeing him again had hurt. She had known that it would. But the pain also confirmed one undeniable fact, she loved Jake Walker. Always would. But she wouldn't have been happy barefoot and pregnant with a horse in the stable and a baby on her hip. Nothing had changed. She needed more from life than that.

But Jake? Jake was tied to the land. He had roots so deep he'd probably die and be buried in the pasture behind the house. He would never leave the land or the horses behind. The dirt and mud were in his blood, in his damn DNA. They just didn't fit.

Which meant leaving him behind to build a new life was still the right choice. And that was a good thing, because she was going to have to say goodbye again in three short weeks.

Claire grabbed her purse and hurried into the brand new hospital complex. She was supposed to meet her mom in the cafeteria in ten minutes. Her dad's shoulder surgery had gone well and he'd be in recovery for a couple hours.

A smiling elderly woman with a giant *Volunteer* sticker on her shirt greeted Claire as she walked up to the information counter. This place was huge, and she had no idea where the cafeteria was.

"Hello, miss. Can I help you?"

"Yes. I need to find the cafeteria."

"Which one?"

What? Since when did hospitals have two cafeterias? "Um, I don't know."

"East wing or west wing, honey?"

"I'm not sure. Just a second, I'll ask." Claire pulled out her phone and shot off a quick text message to her mom. A few seconds later a sound of a bird chirping indicated that her mother had answered. "West."

"Right. You're in the east wing right now." The woman placed a paper map on top of the counter that separated them and began the whole *you are here* speech. Claire got lost after the second elevator switch. She sucked at reading maps.

"Claire? Claire Miller?"

Claire turned to her right and her heart dropped into her shoes. Just what she didn't need, another Walker brother. "Hey, Mitchell." She gave him a once over, and didn't fail to notice that he was still handsome as hell, if you liked the hot, sensual, city-boy type. Tall, dark, and arrogant, that was Mitchell Walker. "So the rumors are true?" She made a point of inspecting his scrubs and white doctor's coat. "They actually let you cut people open?"

"They do." He smiled at her, and his eyes weren't full of anger, or hurt, like Jake's had been. The dark green gaze stared into her soul and she imagined him bent over the operating table, intense and sexy with that lean face and dark hair. The nurses around here probably fought each other just to stand next to him and hand him stuff. Thank God she was immune. She knew too much about Mitchell Walker. He was like a big brother.

"I take it you didn't tell them about how you used to pull the legs off grasshoppers and burn bugs with your magnifying glass?"

"Actually, that was a prerequisite for the job." His smile widened and she smiled back. Mitchell was always fun...trouble, but fun.

"Well, then. The people are in good hands."

He greeted the volunteer and leaned an elbow on the counter to inspect her map. "What are you doing here?"

"I came to check on my dad. He had shoulder surgery this morning. I'm supposed to meet my mom for lunch on the west side."

"Great. I'm just heading over there to do rounds. I'll walk you."

"Thanks."

She thanked the older woman but left the map. If she had to, she'd just go outside and walk around the exterior of the building to get out of here. She preferred open air to this kind of rat maze any day of the week.

The silence felt companionable, so she didn't feel the need to break it. Actually, she kind of hoped to get out of here before Mitchell could grill her for answers. One thing the Walker brothers did do was to watch each other's backs. And her and Jake? Well, they hadn't exactly been a secret. Hell, she'd spent almost as much time with Jake's brothers as he had.

"So, you still living in California?" Mitchell's casual question would be just the beginning and inwardly, she groaned. *Here we go with the Spanish Inquisition.*

"Yep."

"Are you still at UCLA?"

"Technically, yes. I just finished my master's."

"Nice. What did you study?"

"Double major in anthropology and archeology, master's in archeology."

"So that makes you what, Lara Claire Croft, tomb raider?" They waited for the first elevator and she stepped closer to allow more room for a gurney and a wheel chair as the two rolled past pushed by unsmiling hospital staff.

"Not exactly, but I do go out of the country on digs a couple times a year. We spend the rest of the year cataloging and studying the artifacts, or getting them ready for exhibits." She tried not to breathe in too deeply because the smell of hospital antiseptic, medication, and death filled her body with each breath. She hated hospitals. Hated that smell.

"So, what are you going to do after you officially have your degrees? Go for a doctorate?" He reached over and actually pinched her cheek like he used to when she was a little girl. "Are we going to have to call you Professor Miller?"

She slapped at his hand and laughed. "I don't think so. I'm working on a couple of different things, and I'm on a couple of projects that are just waiting for grant approval. UCLA is co-funding an excavation with a state museum. If we get it, we'll be digging at a major Aztec site for a few weeks this coming spring." Museums and universities all over the world were always looking for new projects and new artifacts to exhibit. Claire and Emily had become quite good at researching a museum or university, finding out what they were interested in acquiring, and writing a proposal outlining how they could get it. The money for the excavation trips and study could come from a multitude of sources, anything from a private donor to tax payer funded study grants. The trick was to propose the right idea to the right people, people who were hungry for the idea of an Aztec exhibit, or a new discovery in Pompeii.

The elevator dinged and Mitchell held the door so she could step in first. Immediately she closed her eyes and began to count. She hated elevators. Every time she rode in one she had to talk herself through the science of weights and pulleys. A dark cave, and she was fine. But put her in a man-made contraption, like an elevator or an airplane, and she had to remind herself to breathe.

Mitchell's soft chuckle penetrated her mental mantra. "Still claustrophobic?"

"I'm not claustrophobic, I just hate elevators." She grinned. She couldn't help it, not when he was using his super-charming voice. "Derek still afraid of heights?"

"Terrified, but he'll never admit it." They both laughed and it felt good, like old times. Derek was the oldest Walker brother, dark and brooding and bossy as hell. Derek believed that he ran things and, for most of their early years, his brothers let him. "You should stop by the ranch, have dinner. I'll round up my brothers and you can bring your folks. It would be like old times."

"Uh, thanks. But I think I'll have to take a raincheck. Mom is going to need a lot of help around the house and I don't think dad will be up to it for a while."

Mitchell nodded as the elevator stopped moving and they exited onto their floor. The unmistakable odor of a kitchen reached her and she knew they were close, but not close enough.

"So, have you seen Jake yet?"

She tried, so hard, to keep the blush off her cheeks. "Yep. I dropped off Dad's horses a couple hours ago."

Mitchell was watching her with those intense green eyes, the doctor's eyes, and she felt like he was doing open surgery on her soul...without anesthetic. "I haven't been all the way out there in a while. How's he doing?"

How was he doing? Big, strong and sexier than ever. That was how he was doing. "Um, he's good. He seems good."

"Good." Mitchell grinned and dropped the subject. Thank God.

All four of the brothers had been adopted by Mrs. Walker when they were in grade school. The older three came from shitty backgrounds with drugs, alcohol and abuse. But Jake, he'd just been unlucky. His parents had died in a car crash when he was four and he didn't have any other family to take him. From what she'd gathered over the years, the older three boys treated Jake like their personal little pet until he got old enough to be picked on in earnest. But when their new mother got ahold of them, regardless of their backgrounds, she loved them up and taught them a new way to live. Claire had always admired her for that, and been thankful. Without Mrs. Walker's determination to save her four boys, Claire never would have met Jake. And even though their lives didn't work together, she still would always be grateful for all the fun they'd had over the years.

Mitchell walked with her all the way into the cafeteria, and even stopped for a minute to greet her mother. The Walker boys were always gentlemen, and Claire felt a pang in her chest. She hadn't realized how much she missed home until right now. The Walkers were her family, too. Just as much as her own flesh and blood.

With a promise to check in on her dad, Mitchell left her alone with her mother and Claire slumped into the hard plastic chair with relief. She felt wrung out, like she'd just spent fifteen hours studying for a final and barely passed the test.

"How's Dad?"

"The doctor said the surgery went well and we can go see him in an hour or so." Tears of relief welled in her mom's blue eyes and the sight of them tugged Claire out of her pity party.

"Dad's tough. He'll be up and telling his horrible jokes in no time." Claire reached across the cold, hard surface of the lunch table and grabbed her mom's hand. No one she'd ever met was worse at telling jokes than her dad, and he seemed to have an unlimited supply and enthusiasm for the job.

Her mom chuckled and wiped away the water from both eyes with a napkin from the dispenser that rested in the middle of the table. "He's going to drive the nurses crazy."

Claire smiled. "They'll probably give him extra pain meds just to keep him quiet."

They stood and made their way through the buffet line. Her mom grabbed soup and a baguette while Claire took a chicken sandwich, french fries, some fruit and a brownie. The chocolate was self-medication for the pain of seeing Jake. She knew it, and didn't care. Nope. She took a snicker doodle cookie, too, for good measure.

They sat back down at the table and unloaded their trays. Claire thought maybe her mom was being so quiet and withdrawn because she was worried about Dad. Wrong.

"So, did you take the horses over to Jake this morning?"

"Yes." *And here it comes.* Claire tugged a bleached white napkin from the dispenser and placed it across her lap.

"So, how is he?" Her mom wasn't eating. Why wasn't she eating?

"Good." Claire picked up the brownie and nibbled at the corner. No sense saving it, she needed the sweet explosion of chocolate frosting to give her courage *now*.

"Did you two talk?"

"Yes."

"Did he ask you about California?"

"No. Why would he?"

"Did you tell him you're moving to Denver?"

"I'm not. I just have to take this interview to keep the politicians happy. Dr. Pierson went out on a limb for me, so I have to show up; but I still think it would be better if I take the job at UCLA. And if my grant is approved at the university department's board meeting next week, I'll be out of the country for at least four weeks this spring, and again this coming summer. No man wants a wife who's never around."

"Military families do it all the time."

"Yes, Mom, but I'm not serving my country. I'm doing this for myself. There's a big difference." Claire had the utmost respect for military men and women and their families. They had to deal with separation and sacrifice, but they were answering a higher call, not digging in dirt for the sheer joy of it.

"You need to come home, honey. Settle down."

"No, I don't. Nothing has changed, Mom. Even if I take the Denver job, I'll still be out of the country for weeks at a time. Jake needs a country girl who wants to stay home and make babies, and that's just not me. I'm not sure I want kids at all and I know I don't want them right now." She took a bigger bite of her brownie and gave herself plenty of time to let the chocolate melt on her tongue. When it was gone, she washed it down with a sip of milk and met her mom's worried gaze head-on. "I can't be a rancher's wife. I can't live that life. I'd go crazy. I'd be miserable, and I'd make Jake miserable, too. Nothing has changed since you and I had this exact same conversation seven years ago."

"You're right that nothing has changed. You still love him and I bet he still loves you."

"It's too late, Mom. I can't change who I am, and neither can he. We just want different things."

"I still say it's a mistake, honey. A career can't make you happy."

Claire sighed. "And neither can a man. I need more than that. I can't help it. I just can't do the homemaker thing. And I didn't spend a hundred grand on my education to move out to the ranch and shovel horse shit."

"Claire Leanne Miller, watch your mouth."

"Sorry." Claire kept her hands busy smearing the contents of her mayo and mustard packets onto the top half of the sandwich bun. Claire didn't dare look up, not into those eyes. Her mom knew everything. She saw everything. Claire figured her mom had to be some kind of psychic or something. She should get her own show on cable where she just looked at someone, and they cracked like an egg.

"What do you want me to do, Mom?"

"I just want you to be happy. And Jake loves you."

"That was a long time ago. I'd just make him miserable. He moved on. Got engaged." Claire looked around the cafeteria, at the table, at her food, anywhere but at her mom's face. There were at least twenty people eating in the brightly lit space. Every table had a small vase with a carnation on display. In several windows, stained glass brought a touch of color and beauty to the otherwise sterile room. People were here with loved ones, just like she was. People who had kids dying of cancer, people who had a lot bigger problems than she did. She needed to remember that.

"But it didn't last. Courtney left him, too."

"I didn't leave him, Mom. I let him go. I made sure we could both have the kind of life we wanted." Courtney. God, she hated that name.

"You were a chicken, Claire Miller. That boy loved you. You should have let him make the choice."

"He did choose. He stayed here. He could have gone to California with me, but that wasn't the life he wanted."

"That's not fair to Jake." Her mom harrumphed as if she'd totally won the argument, but Claire wasn't done.

"No, you're not being fair to me. We were seventeen. Nothing matters when you're seventeen. But ten years later? I would have regretted staying. I would have been miserable, and I would have resented him for keeping me here. He wants to live on that land forever and pass it on to kids of his own. Babies, Mom. I can't be a decent mother, not with my job." Heat built behind her eyes, like stabbing hot pokers, and she felt the fiery spill of tears fall onto her cheeks. Crying. She was fucking crying. She'd been back in town less than one full day and she was already losing her mind. "He didn't want to leave the ranch, and I couldn't stay. If I'd stayed, we just would have ended up hurting each other more."

"I think you're wrong, honey. True love is rare. You just have to bend a little."

"No, Mom. There's no middle ground here. Never was. And we both knew it." Claire polished off the cookie and moved on. She dipped a french fry in the ketchup on her plate and stuffed it into her mouth.

She took a bite of chicken, bread, and lettuce. The bread was dry and crumbling, the tomato was white and hard, and the lettuce was so limp it had to be a week old. Claire pretended it was the best thing she'd ever eaten, studied the chicken breast like it was a work of freaking art while her mother stared at her. She could feel those eyes boring into her skull.

"Seventeen-year-olds don't know shit."

Claire choked on her sandwich and had to take a big drink of water to wash it down. Her mother *never* cussed. Ever. "Nothing has changed."

Her mom sighed and stared off into space for a moment. "I understand. It's your life. You have to make the decisions." Her mom tilted her head to the side, and her pale blue eyes pierced Claire like needles straight into her soul. "But you also have to live with the consequences, and so does Jake."

"I know, but this is the way it has to be." Claire wiped at her cheeks with the coarse napkin and cleared her throat. She was done talking about this. Done. Jake wanted ten kids running around in the dirt making mud pies and wading in the creek. He wanted to live and die on the ranch with his horses, a big family, and a wife who loved the ranch as much as he did. That was his dream life, and there was no place in that scenario for a career woman who worked fifty-hour workweeks and spent three months of the year in another country. "He's amazing, Mom. Some brilliant, sexy country girl will fall head over heels in love with him and give him the ten kids he wants. He'll be happy."

"But what if that's not what he wants? What if what he wants is you?"

"I think I burned that bridge."

"I wouldn't be so sure. True love never dies."

"Trust me, it's dead. And I know exactly what Jake wants." Other guys wanted to leave home and go conquer the world. Not Jake. He loved the ranch. For all the years she'd known him, he'd only ever talked about two dreams, a big family and raising horses.

They finished their lunch in silence and Claire was glad. She would go sit with her dad for a while, and then she'd drive back and take a nice long bath. She felt like a cracked piece of glass. One hard push in the right direction, and she'd break into a million pieces.

She had to get out of this state as quickly as possible.

Jake needed a country girl. And someday, he'd fall in love and marry some cute little blonde who baked cookies and knew how to cook, a woman who loved the ranch, loved horses, and got pregnant every time Jake looked at her. Then he'd be happy, he'd have the life he always wanted. It would be perfect.

Claire just couldn't stick around to watch it happen. Knowing she would probably never get married, and never have kids was hard, but she'd come to terms with what her passion for her career was going to cost her. But watching Jake make beautiful babies with another woman?

God, that would be her own personal hell. She was strong enough to walk away and follow her dreams, but she couldn't watch that. That would hurt too much.

Nope. She'd made her choice, and so had Jake. The ranch wasn't her home anymore. She really, really needed to remember that.

Chapter Five

Jake raised his shot glass and waited with the rest of the drunken idiots in the room for Mitchell to finish his toast.

"Drink, for who knows when Cupid's arrow keen, shall strike us and no more we'll here be seen." Mitchell finished his toast and fourteen men raised their glasses with a cheer.

Finally.

Jake raised his glass and tossed back his shot. He had two more empties lined up on the bar next to his beer. Mitchell was wearing his usual expensive pants, city-boy button-down green shirt and a grin. He smelled like an aftershave commercial. What the fuck? Did he dip himself in that shit? And Cupid? When had Mitchell started spouting poetry?

"What the fuck was that?" Derek leaned over and set his empty shot glass on the bar and not for the first time Jake wondered if his oldest brother could read his mind. More often than not, if Jake was thinking it, Derek was saying it.

"Minna Thomas Antrim." Mitchell grinned and Derek slapped him on the side of the head, just hard enough to be annoying, but not start a fight.

"Poetry? This is a fucking bachelor party. You see those strippers?" Derek pointed to the two young women dressed like sexed-up nurses in the middle of the room. "You're supposed to be screaming for tits and beer like a barbarian, not reciting fucking sonnets."

Mitchell raised an eyebrow and leaned against the bar as the bartender set down another round of drinks in front of them. Mitchell wrapped his hand around his glass and swirled the alcohol around until it rotated in a miniature whirlpool. "Tits and beer? I've moved on to blowjobs and whiskey."

"You need to stop fucking everything that moves and find a decent girl to settle down with, like Chance." Derek's suggestion made Jake's head whip around. What the fuck?

"Said the kettle to the pot." Mitchell raised his glass of whiskey and took a sip.

"I don't have time for that shit and I don't need the headache."

"At least get your rocks off, bro. You're going to rub your palm raw with all the action righty must be getting. You must be going broke paying for baby oil and porn subscriptions."

Jake choked on his beer with a laugh at Mitchell's deadpan jibes at their oldest brother. Derek was dressed in the usual black jeans, black T-shirt, black boots, and black attitude. How the hell his brother functioned like that on a day-to-day basis, Jake would never fucking understand. But Derek was reliable, and tough as nails. Jake was glad for that, and just accepted the rest of the bad-boy bullshit that came with it.

Need to hide a dead body? He'd call Derek. Hell, they all would. Derek took care of their messes no matter how dirty the shit got. Jake had kept his nose pretty clean, but Mitchell and Chance had their share of wild days stealing cars, smoking dope, and generally acting like assholes when they were younger. If not for Derek, Jake figured the lot of them probably would have ended up in jail.

Derek turned around to watch their brother, Chance, laugh and slap the groom none of them knew on the back. "He's so fucking happy I can't stand to talk to him."

"Yeah, well, our new sister Erin is hot as fuck." Mitchell spoke the truth about Chance's fiancée and Jake silently agreed. He didn't give a shit what she looked like. She could have warts and purple hair. Erin loved his brother with everything in her. For that, all three of Chance's brothers had her back. She was family now, pure and simple. Officially adopted, which was the best fucking thing that had ever happened to any of the Walker boys. Being adopted was the highest honor they could give her.

Jake swallowed his fourth shot of whiskey and washed away the burn with a sip of his second beer. Normally, he would have stopped after three or four beers. He'd done the shit-faced drunk, passed out and puking thing in college. And he was over it. But tonight, he felt like drowning his sorrows.

Trouble was, the more he drank, the more Claire Miller seemed to expand in his head, until he literally could not think about anything else.

"Give me another one." Jake slid his now empty shot glass back up the bar toward the bartender, who nodded that he'd heard. That was good enough. Jake turned back around to take in the spectacle in front of him. Two women dressed as nurses were dragging Chance, who was the best man, and the groom to the middle of the room. One of Chance's friends from college was getting married next week, and Chance had to put on a penguin suit, try not to lose the ring, and pretend he didn't fucking hate weddings tomorrow night. Tonight's events were all Chance's idea, the bachelor party for his friend. And Chance's three brothers? Hell, they didn't even know the poor sap getting married, they were just along for the ride.

Chance and the groom now sat on chairs in the center of the bar's back room. The strippers were decent looking, with fake tits and too much makeup. Jake figured the nurse outfits had to be Mitchell's idea. Mitchell worked at a city hospital, and it was no secret that he spent a lot of time getting to know the nursing staff.

Derek, plopped down onto his barstool, arms crossed and laughed as Chance was forced by a yelling crowd of drunk Neanderthals to sit down and take his lap dance like a man. The bachelor party wasn't for the groom. Everyone knew that. The drunken debauchery was about grown men and an excuse to party.

Jake leaned his back against the bar and sat with Derek and Mitchell in companionable silence as they watched the first stripper remove handcuffs from her medical bag and lock Chance's hands behind him on the chair. Chance laughed. The groom was up and dancing with the other stripper on the edge of the ring.

Jake turned as the bartender set down another shot of whiskey with the telltale sound of a full glass striking the wooden bar. Derek's gaze pinned him in place like a bug under a needle.

"What you looking at?" Jake knew

he was acting out of sorts tonight, and no, he didn't want to talk about it.

"Hell if I know." Derek sipped on a beer and looked like his typical self, like a one-man Goth squad. He even had his chin-length black hair slicked back on his head, instead of hanging in his face. "What's up with you tonight?"

Jake wasn't touching that one. Time to redirect. "What the fuck did you do to your hair? Your head looks like a wet ball sac."

"Broody and insulting. Now I know something's up." Derek raised his eyebrows as Mitchell returned to them after taking his turn stuffing a five-dollar bill into the g-strings of both strippers. The girls were topless now, one straddling Chance's lap, the other working the crowd for money. Their two brutish bodyguards watched the action from the edge of the room. This party was tame, as bachelor parties went. Poor Chance looked like he was in pain, which made Jake want to laugh. Chance wasn't interested in either of the strippers, other than the usual eye candy. No, his brother was too fucking in love with Erin for that.

Jake wasn't interested either. Since yesterday, he'd only been thinking about one fucking woman. The one he'd been hung up on since grade school. The one woman who he knew, for a fact, had absolutely no interest in him.

Derek smacked him upside the head.

"Ow! What the fuck, man?"

"Am I talking to myself here? I said, what's up with you, Jake?"

Mitchell leaned his elbow against the bar so he could watch the show and eavesdrop at the same time. "Better leave baby brother alone, Derek. Claire Miller's back in town."

"Oh, shit." Derek took a deep breath and braced both hands on the bar in front of him, like he needed the support after hearing such bad news. "Damn it, man. You have *got* to get over that girl."

"I am. She stopped by the ranch yesterday to drop off her dad's horses. That's it. End of story. She's going back to California in three weeks."

"Bullshit, you're over her." Derek flipped back around to watch Chance. Groom and best man now had two bare breasts inches from their faces while their friends howled encouragement.

Jake ignored Derek and turned to Mitchell. "How did you know about Claire?"

Mitchell flagged down the bartender and ordered a burger and fries. He raised his eyebrows at Jake, who shook his head. Not hungry. Mitchell winked at him. "She came by the hospital to check up on her dad." Mitchell waggled his eyebrows at Jake. "She looks fucking amazing. If you're really done with that…"

"Shut the fuck up." Jake knew his brother was just yanking his chain, but he couldn't stop the knee-jerk reaction.

"That's what I thought." Mitchell grinned and reached for beer. "You'll be happy to know, she's not over you either."

Derek snickered. "Now *that's* bullshit. She couldn't leave fast enough."

Jake nodded at his brother to acknowledge the support. Derek wasn't going to fuck around with this, he knew it hurt Jake to damn much. Mitchell, on the other hand, had no fucking mercy at all.

"I asked her about you."

"Jesus Christ, Mitchell. Why the fuck would you do that? She left. Game over." Derek's dark eyes flared with anger and Jake shared that outrage. Claire had looked him in the eye and told him that the life he wanted wasn't ever going to be enough. That summer night, with a full moon shining in her hair and crickets singing under the porch, she had even suggested that he give up the ranch and go with her to California.

Like hell. She should have just asked him to cut off his legs and crawl after her.

He wouldn't leave, and Claire wouldn't stay. So Claire Miller had walked away from him, and the ranch, and his dreams. And she'd never looked back. But there had been something haunted in her eyes the day she left. It was still there.

"What did she say?" Jake couldn't help it. He needed to know. And there was that undeniable masochistic tendency he had when it came to Claire. He just couldn't seem to help himself.

"She didn't say anything. It was the

look on her face. She's still hot for you."

"Bullshit." Derek coughed the word into his closed fist.

Jake wanted details. "Why do you think she's hot for me?"

"You should have seen her face when I asked about you. She blushed. Totally pink in the face."

"That's because she feels guilty for taking off like she did and breaking our boy's heart," Derek said.

"No. I don't think so. I know that look. She wants the cock." Mitchell took a sip of his drink and turned to check on Chance, who was now stuck lying on the floor with both women sitting on him, one on his lap and one on his chest, shaking her tits above his face. Jake just shook his head at Chance's resigned expression. Truth was, some guys liked this stripper shit, and some didn't. Chance and Jake both fell into the *didn't* category.

"You're crude, dude." Jake shook his head in disgust, "and you're wrong."

Mitchell turned his head to face Jake, and he was all kinds of serious. "I'm never wrong about women. She wants you." Mitchell shook his glass so the ice cubes rattled against the side. "Thing is, you want her, too. So, why not have some fun while she's here. Get her out of your system."

"She's only here for three weeks," Jake pointed out.

"Exactly." Mitchell grinned. "You want her. She wants you. You both know the score. So, why not take her for a ride?"

"You're a dick."

"Maybe. But you want to rock that body, or not? I figure, friends with benefits could be a good score for you. Three weeks. Then it's finally over and you can move on. Three weeks and you'll never have to wonder again."

"Wonder what?"

"How hot it would have been if you hadn't ignored your big brother's advice. Don't eat my burger when it comes, you dicks. I'll be right back." Mitchell raised his glass in salute and waded back into the party. But it was too late. Jake knew all he'd be thinking about for the rest of the night was whether or not Mitchell was right about Claire, and about what she wanted from him. And whether or not he had the balls to give it to her.

<><><>

The next morning, Jake stood on his front porch and watched Claire as she led Starlight into the barn on the other side of the property. She looked amazing. A pair of tight jeans hugged her curvy ass and her dark hair had come loose from her braid to frame her face. Her cheeks were flushed, either from the warm morning air or from the excitement of being out on Starlight again. He wished he knew which.

Derek joined Jake on the wraparound front porch in a pair of jeans and bare feet. He held a steaming cup of coffee in one hand and two aspirin in the other. He swallowed the aspirin with a groan and sat down on the front porch swing behind Jake. "Mitchell's wrong. Chasing that tail is nothing but a bad idea, little brother. And it's not just this raging headache talking."

"I know."

"I hate you guys."

Jake turned around to see Derek bend forward with a moan to put his coffee cup on the white wicker table, and his head in his hands.

Jake laughed. "I wasn't the one pouring whiskey down your throat last night."

"No, that was Mitchell. And he should have been picking on Chance. He was the jackass who organized the fucking bachelor party." Derek's black hair was still wet from his shower, and he had traded his black T-shirt for a white one. Real adventurous dresser, his oldest brother.

"Chance had to get to the airport to pick up Erin so they can go to the wedding. Tomorrow they're flying to New York."

"I know. I'm just getting too old for this shit." Derek was twenty-seven, and not much of a partier, not anymore. Most of the time he was too busy in his motorcycle shop to go out, or date, or have a life.

"Just a minute." Jake tracked Claire's every move until she disappeared inside the barn. Once she was out of sight, he went inside the house to pull out the small pitcher of the family hangover cure he had in the fridge. Jake had mixed it for Derek when he heard the shower start. It was Mitchell's recipe and worked pretty well. The brothers never asked the hows or whys, figuring Mitchell's medical degree gave him some kind of magical insight into what a body needed to recover from a night of stupidity.

Jake poured the greenish concoction into two glasses and headed back out to the porch. He took a seat next to Derek on the porch swing and handed his brother a full glass. "Here. Stop whining like a baby."

"Thanks." Derek took his glass and raised it in the air. "A toast. To Chance falling in love. Never thought that motherfucker would fall."

"To Chance. The poor bastard will never get his dick back." And never come home again. Damn. Jake was happy for his brother, but it sucked, too. Chance was the first person Jake used to call when shit hit the fan. Now, he didn't bother. What the fuck was Chance going to do for him from New York or Miami? A couple weeks ago,

Chance and Erin had been all the way up in fucking Canada. Not that Jake didn't love all three of his brothers, but Derek and Mitchell were usually more pain in the ass than sympathetic ear. These days, the only people around Jake felt like he could talk to had four fucking hooves and couldn't talk back.

They clinked their glasses and sipped on the fruity-flavored drink. It was tangy and sweet, with a mixture of juice, greens and vitamins that Jake didn't want to think about. What the fuck was kale, anyway?

Derek sipped at the mixture and tapped out a steady beat on the arm of the swing with his fingertips. "Took a look at the office, Jake."

"Don't start." Jake shoved one hand into the pocket of his down vest and glared at his brother. When their mom died, she'd made sure all the boys got an equal share, and Jake wanted the ranch. It was his now, and so was the responsibility of keeping it running. How he did that was his business.

"You need to hire some help."

"Not this again. I can do it. I just need to spend some time getting caught up."

"You've been saying that since mom got sick." Derek raised his eyebrows. "That was two years ago. And you've got invoices and unopened mail in there that's over a year old. You need help. You can afford to hire someone, so why don't you."

"I just haven't had time, okay? Just, leave it. I'll get to it." Jake was lying and he knew it, but he didn't feel like taking a scolding from his brother right now. That mounting pile of paperwork kept him up nights, but he didn't want a stranger in his house, and none of his field crew could handle the business side. They knew horses and hay, not invoicing and bank reconciliations. He'd gone to college just to learn how to do this shit, so he'd do it. Eventually. He just had to force himself to sit down and go through all of it.

"If you say, so." There was no trace of humor on Derek's face now. "I know you consider that office Mom's sacred space, but she's gone, man. She's been gone for almost a year. It's time to move on. I run a business, and I'm telling you, if you don't get on top of that stack of paperwork, things will get messy."

"I got it. All right? Just back off and give me some space." Jake took a sip of his own green goo and clenched his fist on top of his thigh. Derek was right, that room was his mom's room, and Jake didn't want anyone else in there mucking around. He didn't want anyone else's stuff in there. He didn't want some secretary's purse, or an accountant's coat on the hook. He didn't want anyone to rearrange his mom's filing cabinets or mess up the way she liked to stack the pens and pencils in the drawers. When he was in his house, it still felt like his mom was there, like she would walk around a corner at any given moment and smile. And he wasn't ready to let that go. Not yet. In fact, he hadn't even torn down her bedroom yet, and was still sleeping in his old room instead of the master suite.

Claire was right, he didn't like change.

"So, what are you going to do about your other problem?" Derek drank about half of the green goo and held the half-full glass on top of his thigh. He dropped his head back onto the back of the swing and closed his eyes as if the world were still spinning.

"What other problem?"

Derek snorted, but didn't open his eyes. "Claire."

Jake turned to stare at the outside of the two-story red-and-white barn. The building looked like it could be the star of a country lifestyle magazine. The whole ranch was like that. Trees everywhere. The smell of pine and cool mountain air. Picturesque, that was what Claire had called it when they were in high school. Picture perfect.

And it would have been perfect, if she'd stayed. He would have married her by now, had a couple kids running around screaming and causing trouble. He would have had everything he'd ever wanted, and most importantly, he would have had Claire warming his bed every night.

What was he going to do about Claire?

"Hell if I know. What's with the heart-to-heart?"

"Look, I know Chance isn't here and he's the one you usually talk to about this shit. But, I know you, man. I know you love her." Derek rotated his neck so he could turn to look at Jake without lifting his head. Derek's dark brown eyes looked like pools of near-black. "But she's not staying, Jake. So if you sleep with her, make sure it's for the right reason."

"And what's that?" He should be stronger. He should just tell himself no and walk away. But something about being with Claire the other day had turned him inside out all over again. Then his stupid brother, Mitchell, had to open his fucking mouth and make Jake wonder if Claire still had feelings for him.

Derek sighed and closed his eyes again, returning his head to its stare-up-at-the-ceiling position. "Because you're a fucking masochist and just can't find the will to save yourself a shit-ton of hurt."

Jake sipped his drink again and stared up at the puffy white clouds drifting in a perfect blue sky. "Maybe Mitchell's right and I just need to get her out of my system."

"Mitchell's a moron. Sticking your dick in Claire is just going to make you want her more. And nothing has changed since she left. You still want to live here, raise horses, get married and have kids. She still wants to leave. End. Of. Story."

Jake didn't have an answer for that, at least not one that he could admit to his brother. Wanting her more wasn't possible. He already wanted her so badly he could barely breathe. Sleeping with her again wasn't going to change that, or make it worse. His hunger to touch her couldn't get any fucking worse.

If Derek or Chance had said Claire was still interested, he would have shrugged off his brother's comment about sleeping with Claire as one of the worst ideas in the history of mankind. But Mitchell knew women, he understood exactly what made them tick. They called Jake a horse whisperer. If that were true, then Mitchell was a woman whisperer. He saw things no one else saw. Figured out what women were thinking better than any of the other Walker boys ever could. Asshole. It really wasn't fair.

If Mitchell said Jake had a fighting

chance to be with Claire, then there was a reason. Mitchell must have seen something in her expression, or she'd said something to him.

Jake desperately wanted to know what that something was. Because if Claire still had feelings for him, then everything he'd told himself for the last seven years was wrong. Maybe she was ready to settle down now. Maybe she had changed her mind about coming home. Maybe she'd seen enough of the world. Maybe.

At seventeen, she'd broken his heart. Oh, he realized immediately that he'd missed all the signs. She had applied to more than a dozen schools out of state. She'd talked nonstop about traveling the world. And she'd kept him at arm's length until he'd pushed her. He'd been so fucking tired of being stuck in the friend zone that he'd forced the issue. He'd kissed her, and she'd given in. He knew she loved him. That was a given. But he'd thought when he took her virginity that she'd stay, like having sex was going to magically tie her to him and keep her from leaving town, keep her from going off to school.

He'd naively thought having sex would make her dream about a life with him, instead of a life of her own.

Way fucking wrong on that one. It just made her leaving hurt more for both of them. Too late he understood that she'd been trying to protect him. But then, Claire had always been smarter than he was about a lot of things.

"Well, I guess I crave pain. I'm going to go talk to her."

"It's your funeral." Derek stood up and grabbed his half-full coffee cup off the table. "I'm outta here. I've got three custom jobs waiting for me." He tipped the empty green glass to his brother. "Thanks for letting me crash out here."

"You were too drunk to drive home."

"Yeah. Which means my Jeep is still at the bar. Can you give me a lift into town?"

"Sure. Just give me a few minutes."

"I'll give you ten. You can finish up and put it back in your pants by then, right?" Derek grinned and Jake stacked his empty glass on top of Derek's so his big brother would have to take it into the kitchen.

"You're not helping."

"I tried. Not my fault you're a pussy-whipped moron."

"Asshole." Derek's grin was infectious, but Jake waited for his brother to disappear inside the house before heading for the barn. No need for an audience to witness this train wreck.

Claire had the barn doors closed and it took his eyes a minute to adjust to the dim light once he stepped inside. The horses were all comfortable and snug in their stalls with full oat buckets. Mindy must have just fed them all breakfast.

He searched the barn for the older woman, but it was empty now except for the horses, and Claire. He heard her before he saw her. The tip of a brush peeked out over the top of Starlight's back, traveled along the horse's side and disappeared. Claire crooned to the horse as she brushed her down, and the soft sound of Claire's voice stirred up trouble. The longer he listened, the harder he got.

Jake moved silently through the center aisle, grateful that the horses on both sides of him were too busy eating to give him their usual greeting. He came up even with Starlight's stall and leaned against the wood beam opposite the gate with his arms crossed over his chest. Watching. Listening. Waiting.

He would just wait here and talk to her, see if he could figure out what Mitchell was talking about. Maybe he just needed to push her a little bit, get her riled up.

Maybe a kiss or two would rattle her super-tight control...

Chapter Six

Claire hummed softly to Starlight as she finished brushing the mare's gorgeous mane and fed her the last apple slice she had kept hidden in the pocket of her hoodie. The cool morning air bit at her hands and cheeks like long-lost friends. She missed this dry air and the change in seasons. Southern California was beautiful, but every day was the same— sunny, warm enough for shorts, and predictable. It had been seven years since she'd been surrounded by the smell of hay, and horses, and morning air so crisp that it smelled like ice, even in the summer. The mountain peaks were still coated with a white layer of snow and snow clung to the edges of ditches and in the shade on the north side of the bigger tree trunks. She'd missed the smell of pine trees and sage, and snow.

"I missed you, too, girl." She rubbed Starlight's nose and patted her on the shoulder as she put the brush away in the bag that hung from the side of the large enclosure. Starlight's bucket and water were full and there was nothing else to do here, no more excuses she could use to delay driving home. No more dragging her feet in the idiotic hopes that she might catch a glimpse of Jake.

She opened the paddock and stepped out into the center of the barn, walking backward so she could pull the gate closed behind her. "I'll see you tomorrow."

Starlight whinnied and stuck her big head over the top of the gate to get in the last word. Claire felt a bittersweet joy at being with the horse again. "I know, girl. I'm sorry. I wish I could stay longer."

"Then why don't you?" Jake's question had her whipping around to look for him, and hoping she was just hearing things. No such luck, the big, handsome cowboy stood less than three steps away, looking every bit as sexy as she remembered in boots, jeans, and a layered plaid shirt with just enough blue to bring out the matching shade in his eyes. His face peeked out from beneath the brim of a tan cowboy hat and his jeans hugged his rock-hard thighs like a second skin. He was straight up fantasy material. And he was talking to her.

"What?" Claire took a step back and bumped into Starlight's stall. "Hi, Jake. I didn't know you were out here."

"Obviously, because that's the first time I've heard the real Claire talking since you came home."

"This isn't my home, Jake. Not anymore."

"Why haven't you come back to visit? Seven years, and you never even came home for Christmas." Jake was leaning back with his arms crossed over his chest and one knee bent. He used his bent leg to push off from the wooden beam so he could take a step toward her. "You afraid to see me again? Feeling guilty?"

"No. I'm not afraid of you. We broke up. That's all." Claire shoved her hands into the pockets of her hoodie to make sure Jake couldn't see them shaking. "It happens all over the world, every single day."

"You never were a good liar, Claire. You've been avoiding me for seven years. Why is that?" He moved closer, and with a couple inches of height added by his boots, his six-four frame towered over her. God, he was hot. And big. And so beautiful it hurt to look at him.

She would have backed away, but she didn't have anywhere to go. Starlight's latched gate pressed into her back and the big, stupid horse's head came down to rest on her left shoulder in solidarity. It was like the big horse knew she needed a friend right now. Female support.

Jake closed the distance between them until he was close enough to reach up over her shoulder and pet Starlight's head. Her horse neighed and talked to Jake like he was an old friend. The traitor.

When Jake had greeted the horse, and stolen all the air from the small space that separated them, he returned his attention to her, and she wished he hadn't. His baby-blue eyes, usually so open and calm, ready to laugh, were hard and demanding. "What is going on with you, Claire? Are you trying to drive me crazy?"

She was driving *him* crazy? Claire took a deep breath in an attempt to gather her wits, but realized that was the very worst thing she could have done as the scent of pine and leather, of Jake, filled her head and clouded her senses. He smelled so good, she just wanted to press her face to his neck and breathe him in for hours.

Jake dropped his right hand from the horse and shifted so that he had her trapped, with one arm on each side of her head. She was tall, used to looking most men in the eye, even looking down at a few, but Jake loomed over her, and his barely suppressed anger radiated from his body like heat waves. She could literally *feel* the intensity of his emotions swirling beneath the surface.

His face was so close that all she had to do, if she wanted to kiss him, was *lean* a little. Just a few inches. And with that traitorous thought, her gaze dropped to inspect his mouth.

God, she'd missed his mouth.

"Claire?"

"What?" She lifted her gaze and was caught by the heat and attention she saw in his eyes. He was one-hundred-percent focused right now, on her.

"Are you going to answer me?"

"I'm not doing anything, Jake." She dropped her gaze to his chest because she knew she was about to lie to him again, and she couldn't look him in the eye while she did it. "We broke up. I left. I'm sorry it didn't work out between us."

Jake leaned closer, until his lips grazed her cheek as he asked his next question. "And now? Could things work out now?"

"Now what? Nothing's changed." Oh, shit. Where was he going with this? And why couldn't she find the strength to tell him to get the hell off her and let her go.

Because in his arms was exactly where she wanted to be.

"And you're leaving in three weeks?" He whispered the question against her ear and the heat of his breath sent a shiver across her skin.

"Yes. I'm leaving in three weeks."

"So, give me three weeks, Claire."

"What?" She was going to hyperventilate if her heart tried to race any faster. Or worse, it would pound so loudly Jake would hear it.

He lifted his hands off the gate and slid them behind her back. When she looked up, their gazes locked and he pulled her body closer and closer, until they were hip to hip and chest to chest. His erection was solid and eager to greet her, and she held back a groan as her body went up in flames at the intimate contact.

Her mind could scream all it wanted to, but her body knew these arms and this smell. Her core clenched with need as the memories of Jake's thick length stretching her surged to the forefront of her awareness. It had been seven long years, but she could remember every touch of Jake's big hands, every caress of his lips, every sensation like it was yesterday.

Helpless to deny herself the pleasure of being in Jake's arms, she didn't resist or push him away.

She knew what was coming, and wanted it so badly she would have sold her soul to get it.

And then, it happened. Jake pressed his lips to hers and she was too starved for his touch to remember all the reasons she shouldn't kiss him back.

With a soft cry, she wrapped her arms around his neck and opened to his kiss as he tasted and explored her. He kissed her like a man starved for the taste of her, a man who needed her touch as much as he needed air.

It went on and on, until Claire was dizzy and panting, and unable to think. At last, he broke off the kiss and they rested with their foreheads pressed together and the hot air between their lips mingling in the space between their lips.

"I want you, Claire."

She stiffened and tried to pull back, but he refused to let her go, and his arms were strong as steel behind her back. "No, way. I can't do this. I'm leaving in three weeks."

"I know. But you still want me. And I want you. We're single. Free. Let's just get this thing out of our systems." He kissed her again, a soft lingering kiss on her lips and she sighed when he pulled away. "Ever heard of friends with benefits?"

"But...?" Before she could string three words together, Jake kissed her again.

"Don't think about it, Claire. Just be with me. Three weeks. That's all I'm asking. No strings. No bullshit. Just sex."

"I'm leaving, Jake."

"I know." He leaned in close and kissed her on the nose, "but you make me crazy. We're explosive together. The sex would be intense. And I want you in my bed, even if it's only for three weeks."

"It won't matter how many orgasms I have, I won't change my mind. I can't stay. We still want different things, Jake. Our lives just won't work together." Claire's heart was pounding and the argument going on between her heart and her head had escalated into a complete mental meltdown. Her head wasn't going to win this one.

"I know. I'm not asking for anything more. Just three weeks. I promise."

Claire shook her head. This was insane. "I don't know."

Jake kissed her cheek and stepped back. "Think about it, okay? Go riding with me tomorrow morning. You can ride Starlight and I'll take out Widowmaker. You can let me know what you want to do tomorrow."

Claire nodded and made a run for it. Jake, all hers, for three weeks, with no strings? If she stayed one more minute in that barn, she'd throw Jake down in the hay and climb all over him like a nymphomaniac.

It would hurt when she left, but leaving was going to rip her heart out anyway. Just like last time.

But three weeks with Jake? She already knew what her answer was going to be. She had never stopped loving him. She wanted him every way she could get him. And this was an offer she wasn't stupid enough to refuse.

<><><>

Claire bent lower over Starlight's neck and tried to outrun the big stallion chasing them, and the sexy cowboy in the saddle. She grinned back over her shoulder and laughed when she saw him pull up on his reins to let her win.

Their horses' hooves pounded on the hard, dry ground like miniature thunderstorms as she raced Jake back to the stables. Starlight was fast, but she was twelve years older than the stallion, and shorter. Widowmaker had to carry a lot more weight. Jake was six-four and thick across the chest and back. He was strong, so strong that he used to lift her over his head and toss her in the hay before he kissed her. And she wasn't exactly a small woman.

That strength was just one more thing she loved about him, one more thing she was going to miss when she left.

Back at the stable, they worked quickly and efficiently to take care of the horses and gear. Falling back into the old rhythm was so easy, so comfortable. He took the saddles, she took the tack. He checked the horses' legs and overall health while she fed them treats and talked nonsense to them.

So familiar. So perfect. But then,

everything with Jake had always felt like home to her.

Jake. Since that kiss in the barn yesterday, she'd been unable to eat, or sleep, or think about anything but being with him again. Even now, in the cool morning air, with her hands going numb inside her gloves, her cheeks burning in the wind, and her legs screaming in pain because it had been so long since she'd gone riding on a regular basis, she was hot, so damn hot for Jake Walker.

When they finished up and had both horses taken care of, Jake gave her that look and she stood still as a statue as he closed the distance between them.

"Come on. Let's go inside."

"Okay."

He took her by the hand and led her up to the big house and inside, to the mudroom next to the back door. They both hopped around, taking off their boots, which were covered with mud from the creek, horseshit, and hay. Jake helped her out of her hoodie, yanking it over her head when she got stuck, and hung it on a wooden peg as she stuffed her hat and riding gloves into a cubby just above it.

"Hot chocolate?"

"How about coffee?" She needed caffeine, not sugar.

Jake raised an eyebrow. "Are you sure? I have marshmallows."

"I'm sure."

"Come on." Jake pulled her along by the hand to the large, open kitchen. The island in the center was bare except for a knife block and built-in cutting board next to a stainless steel sink where they both washed their hands. The cabinets were a golden oak and the counters a swirl of brown, gray and yellow marble. The room was bright and cheery, just like Mrs. Walker had been.

Claire ran her hand along the smooth marble counter and smiled. "This was always my favorite room. It reminds me of your mom." Jake's mother had spent countless hours baking and scolding her boys in this room. The plain wooden table and chairs still held its place of honor on the far side of the kitchen next to a big bay window. Claire had spent many happy hours sitting next to Jake at that table doing homework, struggling with quadratic equations, or spearing helpless insects with needles for a science project.

"Me, too. She practically lived in here." Jake smiled at her over the top of the coffee pot. He measured out a few heaping spoonfuls of ground coffee into the machine and turned it on. The sharp tang of coffee filled the air as he got two large mugs out of the cabinet. Claire kept her hands occupied by walking over to the pantry and grabbing the sugar. Once she set that down, she opened the drawer and selected two spoons.

She still knew where everything was. The silverware and the wineglasses. The spice rack and the baking sheets. "Everything is still in the same place."

"Mom didn't like change."

Claire chuckled when she saw a stack of unopened mail was still kept in the same basket, on the same corner of the counter. "Neither do you." He didn't like change. Jake liked comfortable old slippers, worn-out quilts. He didn't like a new pair of boots until he'd worn them for at least six months, and he'd used the same deodorant and the same cologne since he was thirteen.

"That's true." Jake poured two cups of coffee and stepped close to hand one of them to her. "I don't know how you take your coffee. You didn't use to drink it."

Trembling slightly, Claire took the cup and soaked in the warmth of being so close to him. Her toes were cold and the tile floor wasn't helping her feet warm up. "I'll do it. Thanks."

As Jake watched every move, Claire measured two heaping teaspoons of sugar into her mug and topped it off with the half and half Jake handed to her when he was finished with it. She held up the sugar dispenser, but he shook his head.

"No thanks. I'm already sweet enough."

Claire took a sip of her own coffee and sighed with bliss. Hot coffee. Jake's kitchen. Jake. This felt like home again, like old times, at least for the moment.

"Come on." Jake tilted his head toward the family room and Claire followed him into the homey space she knew almost as well as her own home.

Two large couches sat opposite each other with a rectangular table between them. A large fireplace took up half the wall at one end of the room, and a giant television hung from the wall on the other side. Southwestern-style blankets had been hung over the couch backs and the room was decorated with horses in all forms, small statues, hanging on the walls, and woven into the area rug that covered the floor.

In the center of the table stood a lone, empty soda bottle.

"Is that...?" Holy shit. Had he *kept* it?

"Yes."

"Oh, no." Claire took a step back, but too late. Jake closed the double glass doors behind her, shutting them in the room. The windows were hung with one-way sheers and the glass doors were covered with blinds. They would be completely alone. Even if any of his crew came into the house from outside, they wouldn't be able to get in. Claire knew, because she'd given Jake her virginity on that rug seven years ago.

And just like that night, so long ago, Jake clicked the lock on the door, throwing Claire's mind into a flashback. Hot bodies writhing on the floor in front of the fireplace. Jake covering her body, taking her innocence as she took his, both of them too overcome with emotion to talk. She closed her eyes to block out the image of the fireplace, but that was the wrong thing to do. The room smelled like leather and...*him*.

"This was a bad idea." Claire's voice rang with panic and there wasn't a thing she could do about it. Alone. With Jake.

Jake froze. "So, is that your answer? No?"

Claire walked to the couch and sat down. She put her coffee cup on the table, right next to that long-necked soda bottle that had helped her give herself to Jake all those years ago. She stared at the glass bottle for a minute. She still wanted Jake. She'd known being with him was going to hurt. But now, it was time to adjust and get things moving. She could either sit here reminiscing about the past and everything she'd lost...or she could spin that bottle and get Jake naked.

She reached over and laid the bottle down onto its side. With a flick of her wrist she sent it spinning in a perfect circle. "Sit down, Jake."

"You still remember the rules?" Jake abandoned his post at the door and sank down next to her on the couch, just like the last time.

"West side of the table is me, east side is you." When the bottle stopped spinning, it was pointing right at her and she actually closed her eyes in anticipation as Jake whispered the question that had cause her heart all the trouble she could handle. Just three words. They weren't *I love you*, but these three words were very powerful, and much more dangerous at the moment.

"Truth or dare?"

Chapter Seven

Jake set his coffee mug down on the other end of the table and waited for her answer. *Truth or dare?*

"Dare."

That was the answer he wanted, and he couldn't stop the grin from spreading across his face, or the hard-on coming to life in his pants. "Crawl onto my lap and straddle me."

She raised an eyebrow, but got up from where she'd been perched on the edge of the couch and moved to stand in front of him. "You are a dangerous man, Jake Walker."

"Right here." Jake leaned as far back in the couch cushion as he could get and patted his thigh as he waited, like an overeager teenager, for the woman of his dreams to climb onto his lap. This was just how things had started between them last time. Exactly the same. Then he'd kissed her, and all hell had broken loose inside him. And just like that fateful night seven years ago, he'd planned ahead. He had two condoms in his pocket and a soft blanket tucked away, ready to spread out on the floor in front of the fireplace.

Claire settled her hands on his shoulders as she assumed her position on his lap. They faced each other now, and a hint of orange teased him from the braid that rested on her shoulder. He ached to touch her and couldn't resist the urge to run his hands up and down the outside of her thighs. He wanted to reach around, grab her ass and haul her body up tight against his erection, but he waited, savoring the moment.

"Now what?" Her dark brown eyes dropped to his lips, but he denied them both. Not yet. He was having too much fun.

"My turn."

"You can't reach the bottle." She grinned down at him and he smiled back.

"Then, I guess you'll have to reach

over and spin it for me."

"Don't let me fall." Her teasing gaze locked with his as she leaned back, arching her back away from him, to reach the bottle on the table and set it spinning. The hem of her shirt rode up to just above her waist and Jake couldn't resist moving his hand to the bare skin at her waist to support her weight.

"Have I ever?"

Her eyes clouded and she looked away, watching the bottle whirl on the table. Wrong thing to say, dumb ass. He'd hurt her before, by pushing, just like he was doing now. She'd tried to hold him at arm's length back in high school, tried to keep their relationship platonic, but he hadn't been happy with that. He'd wanted more. He'd wanted *her*.

But ranch life and her career ambitions didn't mesh. He knew that. He'd always known that. But he'd wanted what he wanted, and like a seventeen-year-old, shortsighted idiot, he'd gotten exactly what he wanted…Claire, naked and hotter than the fire that had blazed on the grate the night he'd taken her.

The sound of the bottle whirring on the hardwood table filled the room. He stared at the delicate curve of her jaw and the soft curve of her lips for a moment before watching the bottle as it came to a stop. She shifted her weight and he stifled a groan as her center pressed down, hard, on his lap.

"Truth or dare, Jake?" Her breathless question made his pulse kick up a notch. And as much as he wanted to know what she might dare him to do next, he also really needed to know what was going on in her head. For ten years, she'd told him everything. Everything. Then he'd been stupid and impatient and ruined everything. He wasn't that arrogant young asshole anymore. He just had to convince her that they could be friends again, that she could trust him again.

"Truth."

Claire's head whipped around and she stared at him, taking her time to consider her question. She only got one. Those were the rules. The look in her eyes deepened from aroused to serious.

"Why are you doing this, Jake?"

Oh, shit. The Claire he'd known at

seventeen never would have asked him that question head-on. How the hell was he supposed to answer without either scaring her off, or sounding like an asshole? Dumb. He should have taken a dare.

Holding her gaze, he lifted his hands to frame her face before gently pulling her toward him. Redirect. That was his only safe option, because somewhere between that scorching-hot kiss in the barn yesterday and this moment he'd realized the truth.

The truth was the diamond solitaire in the top drawer of his dresser in a black velvet box. He wanted her to come home. He wanted her to stay.

Was it foolish? Irrational? Impossible? Yes. All those things, but he couldn't tell her that. His heart didn't care. When it came to Claire, his heart had always ruled his head. Some things never changed.

"This is why." Jake pulled her to him and claimed her lips. He didn't hold back, not this time. In the barn, he'd been afraid to scare her. But now, he put seven years of longing in his kiss. He wanted her to know what desperation tasted like.

Claire wrapped her arms around his head and gave him everything he wanted. She opened to him and allowed him to taste and explore, to plunder and claim. Every primal instinct he had roared to life as he held her in place and demanded surrender.

But she wasn't an inexperienced girl this time, and she pushed back, her tongue and lips meeting his passion thrust for thrust. She gave, and she demanded in equal measure, the ebb and flow of submission and aggression tuned his entire body to hers until the world faded away. He no longer felt the couch at his back or heard any noise but the shuddering gasps that escaped her lips. When her hands found their way to the buttons of his shirt, he had no intention of resisting her.

Reaching up to her shirt, his shaking hands fumbled with her buttons until he got the first three down. Impatient, he grabbed the hem and lifted it over her head to reveal her soft pink camisole. When she would have reached for his shirt again, he tugged at her until she lifted her arms again and he could pull the thin stretchy fabric over her head as well. He dropped the shirts, forgotten, on the floor at the sight of her lacy pink bra and bare shoulders. So much skin, and he wanted to taste every single inch.

He leaned forward and nibbled his way along her collarbone to her neck, encouraged by her soft sigh as she let her head fall back to give him more access.

Hell, yeah.

"I want you, Jake."

He didn't answer, just kissed and sucked on her soft skin until she squirmed her way off his lap.

"What...?" Jake reached for her but she stopped him with a slight shake of her head. Sexy as hell, she reached up and unwound her hair from the braid until the long dark waves fell past her shoulder like a goddess come to life. Grinning at him now, she unhooked her bra and let it fall to the floor next to her shirt. He grabbed for her again, and she caught his hands, lifting them to cup the heavy weight of her full breasts. He traced her nipples with his thumbs, eager to pull her back down onto his lap, but her hands fell to her waist and she yanked down her jeans to stand naked before him.

Holy shit.

"I said, I want you."

Jake kneaded her breasts, satisfied with the way she pressed forward, into his touch. "I'm right here."

"Right now." She dropped to her knees in front of the couch and reached for the button off his jeans. She eyed him like he was her favorite candy as he yanked both layers of shirt off, over his head in one fast, efficient move while she unbuttoned and unzipped his pants. When she tugged, he lifted his hips and helped her get him as naked as she was.

He was ready to move to the floor, or pull her down with him on the long couch, but Claire had other plans.

Claire was impatient, barely shoving his pants down around his ankles before her mouth closed over the head of his penis like a jolt of liquid lightning. He froze at her touch. God help him, he couldn't resist, not when she sucked the sensitive head into her mouth and tongued him, not when she used her free hands to squeeze his nipple and play with his balls.

He let her have her way until he couldn't take it anymore. He wanted to be inside her. He wanted to touch…

"Claire. Stop." Jake groaned when she ignored him, taking him deeper, until his hard length bumped the back of her throat and he nearly lost control. He buried his fingers in her hair and pulled at her head until she lifted her mouth from him. "Jesus, Claire."

She grinned up at him. "Let me guess, condom in your left front pocket?"

Not waiting for an answer, she searched his jeans pocket for the condom and lifted it triumphantly. "I knew it."

Shock held him still. Was he really that predictable?

Before he could recover from that thought, Claire rolled the condom over him and was climbing back up into his lap. "Claire, this isn't…"

"What? You don't want this?" Straddling him now, Claire's forehead pressed to his as she tilted her hips and rubbed her wet heat over the top of his hard length. She sank down onto him, so that just the tip of his hard length entered her body. "Do you want me to stop?" She breathed the question with her lips grazing his.

Did he want her to stop? Hell, no. But this wasn't the way he'd imagined things between them. This wasn't what he'd had in mind, but he wanted her to take every hard inch as deep as he could go.

"Don't stop. Ride me." There was only so much he could take, and his brain was ruining the moment for his dick. Not cool.

Claire impaled herself on his hard length and he let her go slow, knew he was big. She slid down and up a couple of times, testing the ride, and his limits.

This wasn't the Claire he remembered, soft and sweet and innocent. The girl who'd let him take control. The softhearted girl who'd taken his heart with her when she left.

When he knew she could handle him, he let go of his restraint and claimed her lips as he thrust up into her for the first time. He stole her soft cry from her mouth and sank his hands into her hips to pull her body closer to his, so the angle would rub her against his abdomen in just the right spot to make her come apart. She hadn't let him taste her, she hadn't let him explore or play.

He would remedy that next time. But right now, she wouldn't deny him her release.

They rocked against each other, too hard, too fast, like two runaway trains unable to change tracks or stop. She whimpered, so close, and he knew he wasn't going to last long enough to take her with him so he reached down between their bodies and stroked her, rough and fast. With a sharp cry, she pulsed around his hard length as her orgasm ripped through her, taking him right over the edge with her.

He wrapped his arms around her back and held her still on his lap, kissing her over and over because he had to, because he couldn't get enough, because he couldn't face her, not yet. When the loving stopped, he'd have to look her in the eye and let her walk out of here.

And too late, he knew both of his brothers had been right. Claire wanted him, all right. But his oldest brother's prediction was the one that stung. As usual, Derek's hard-ass words had been the truth. He sat, buried balls deep in a woman he realized he barely knew. The innocent, starry-eyed girl he'd fallen in love with was long gone.

And the woman who'd just rolled over him, who'd just taken exactly what she wanted?

Claire was all grown up, sexy, and hotter than he'd ever imagined.

And he was in deep, deep shit.

Chapter Eight

Cell phone buzzing in her purse, Claire pulled it out discreetly and glanced at the message. She was in the middle of a job interview and she knew she should ignore it, but she found that she couldn't resist. She'd known, even before she looked, that the text would be from Jake. Yesterday, she had gone a little wild on him, a bit primal. But he hadn't seemed to mind. No, he'd dug his big, strong hands into her hips and pulled her down on top of him. Hard and fast, just like she wanted.

Want to go for another ride?

On you? Or the horses? She hit the send button and grinned. Where had this naughty side come from? Jake seemed to be the only one who could bring it out of her.

Horses first. Then me. I'll take longer.

The grin morphed into an all-out smile before she could stop it. Tomorrow was Tuesday, and she was completely free. Her fingers flew over the screen. *Tomorrow. 9:00.*

What if I want to ride you?

Claire wanted to shout "Yes!" at the top of her lungs, but didn't dare. Yes—on the floor, in the barn, over the back of the couch, in the shower, from behind while she was on her hands and knees in his bed, in that rug in front of his fireplace—yes. She controlled herself and typed three letters. *Yes.*

I get to taste you first. Claire's feet stopped moving as her whole body shouted another gigantic freaking 'yes' to that. Heat spread through her at the thought of his mouth on her, but she didn't respond. Instead, she put the phone on airplane mode and shoved it back into her purse, thankful that Dr. Levinson hadn't caught her with her phone out. She hurried to catch up to the man giving her a tour of the museum's basement levels. Jake was a distraction, a hot, sexy, totally inappropriate distraction, and she couldn't afford to be preoccupied at the moment.

Claire's high heels struck the polished museum floors in a steady beat as she followed the museum's top dog in the antiquities department through the labyrinth of art and artifacts that the public never got to see. The musty smell of ancient relics, dust, and wooden storage crates wrapped around her, the scents and sights familiar and comforting.

"As you can see, we have a good start on the Pompeii exhibit expansion, but we need to acquire more pieces before we can finalize construction plans." Dr. Levinson was wearing a pair of khakis and a red polo, both of them coated with dust from whatever project her interview was interrupting. Dr. Levinson was pushing sixty, but his eyes were bright and he had a sharp wit. He also had a Ph.D. from Yale and had logged more than twenty years of field experience. He'd lived Claire's dream life already, and this tour had made her hungry to get back out in the world and get dirty.

"It's amazing. You know, my colleague Emily Davis and I actually submitted a research proposal to the museum trust last year on Herculaneum." The town was lesser known than Pompeii, but had been destroyed by the same deadly volcanic blast that wiped out three cities. And, she'd always wanted to go to Italy.

"I didn't know that. Fantastic. Have you heard anything?"

"No, but I didn't really expect to. It was a long shot."

"I see. Let me show you the rest." Dr. Levinson pointed out a few of their more stunning pieces for the exhibit, including a plaster casting of two bodies taken in 1864 from buried remains in Pompeii by the famous archeologist Giuseppe Fiorelli. The casts were made from bodies found at the sight and were nearly perfect in their detail, from the expression on the deceased's face to their clothing. The sight of such naked anguish made Claire wrap her arms around herself and shiver.

"How did you get these? I didn't think they allowed the castings to leave the country."

"Ah, they are replicas on loan from the archeological department there." He grinned at her. "I have some very good friends in Naples, my dear."

"Wow. I guess. These are amazing."

"I knew you would appreciate them."

Claire had already answered all the questions, submitted her credentials via email and jumped through all the hoops. She'd applied for the job because Dr. Howard Pierson, the lead on her dig in Brazil, had recommended her to Dr. Levinson. It would have been rude, and bad politics, not to follow through with the application. As soon as she'd told the team that she was flying home to Denver and would be in town for a while, Dr. Pierson had made his call. With Dr. Pierson's personal recommendation, and her extensive fieldwork for someone her age, this interview was a formality — and they both knew it. The job in acquisitions was on the table, the question was whether or not Claire was going to take it. A week ago, she hadn't even considered the possibility of moving to Denver. But a week ago, she hadn't been home, or hooked up with Jake.

Dr. Levinson completed her tour

through the lower levels and Claire grew more impressed. The museum was huge, the largest in the central part of the country, and had a remarkable number of exhibits and artifacts. But no museum was ever satisfied with what they had in the vaults. They always wanted more. Something new and exciting. Something to keep the public walking through the doors and the donors signing checks.

"Thank you for the tour, Doctor, I am impressed."

Dr. Levinson led her into his tiny office and sat down across from her behind a desk not much bigger than most school children used. "I knew you would be. This is a good place to be, Claire. I hope you'll consider joining our team."

Claire stood, ran her sweaty palms down her skirt to make sure it was straight, and held out her right hand. "Thank you. I appreciate your time, and the generous offer, but I need some time to think about it. I'm just not sure I'm ready to give up field work yet."

"Oh, yes. I understand completely." Dr. Levinson rose and shook her hand, his grip warm and friendly, and his smile one of complete accord. He pumped her hand up and down in the air with enthusiasm. "I know what it's like to be young and free. I know what it's like to love getting three-thousand-year-old dirt under your nails. The excitement of discovering something new."

"Yes. Thank you." She released his hand and stepped back, wrapping both hands around the strap of her purse to keep them from shaking. This job wasn't in the cards for her. Dr. Levinson was great. The museum was amazing, but she would have to give up fieldwork, give up traveling to exotic new places, be stuck behind a desk in a basement for the rest of her life. No way. "I will think about your offer."

"Excellent. We aren't making an official decision for a couple weeks, so you have some time to think about it. We'll be in touch."

Claire nodded and left his office, hurrying down the hall to the elevators that would take her back up and outside. She needed some fresh air.

Taking this job would ruin her

plans. And she still had three other proposals under review. If one of those hit, she'd be on a jet as soon as she could pack her bags. She couldn't commit to this desk job. No way.

But I could have Jake.

Claire wiped a stray tear from her cheek as the elevator doors dinged and she stepped inside. Where had that come from?

This wasn't about Jake. This was about her. She'd been to several countries, including Egypt, and she wanted to go back. And there were at least two-dozen countries around the world she wanted to explore. Putting down roots and settling into the traditional role of marriage and changing diapers just didn't appeal to her. Maybe in ten years. Maybe not. And she couldn't ask Jake, or any other man, to wait that long when she wasn't sure she would ever change her mind.

She loved the hunt, loved traveling, loved exploring the world. And she just wasn't ready to hang it up, not yet. Her career was important to her, seeing the world, exploring new archeological sites. She'd left behind the only man she'd ever loved for her career. She wasn't about to give up her dreams for a desk buried in a small room in a museum basement. She might as well be one of those ancient relics down there, collecting dust and left to rot.

And as much as she talked herself in circles, the whole thing was just depressing. She loved Jake. Always had. Probably always would. But simply having a man and starting a family would never be enough for her. Some women wanted that life, and she admired them for it. Raising a family was hard, and she knew that. The emotional and physical toll was one she definitely respected, which was why she had decided that kind of life just wasn't in the cards for her. Would she love to have children, and a husband? Maybe someday. But that simply was not her top priority. She needed more.

She could see it now, her and Jake, married with four kids. She'd have a big blue-eyed baby on one hip and three more adorable little ones sitting at that big table in Jake's kitchen, coloring or doing homework. She'd be cooking something for dinner, doing laundry, and feeding the baby a bottle all at the same time. Her hair would be limp from not having showered for three days, she'd be carrying an extra twenty pounds of baby weight that she never had time to work off, and the circles under her eyes would be deep and not covered by makeup. Her biggest adventure of the week would be leaving the ranch and dragging four kids to the grocery store without either losing track of one of them, or killing one of them, and her only adult conversation would be with her husband for one hour a night between the time the kids went to bed and she passed out from exhaustion watching the Discovery Channel as they broadcast television specials that highlighted ancient relics, tombs, and archeological sites that she'd never actually get to see.

Twenty years down the road, she would still love Jake, and their kids. But a part of her would hate them, too. A deep part of her would swell with discontent, then anger, and finally she would grow to resent Jake, and the kids, and their life together.

No fucking way she could do that to

him, or to herself. Or to their totally hypothetical, but adorable, future children. That would be cruel, and selfish, and just stupid. Children needed two parents who loved them and were happy they existed. Not a mother who looked at them and just saw opportunities lost and sacrifices made.

No, she knew who she was and what she needed. And no matter how amazing the orgasms were with Jake, hot sex with a gorgeous cowboy wasn't enough for her, no matter how much she loved him.

The elevator stopped moving and she walked with brisk strides to her dad's big truck. The cold wind and spitting bits of frozen rain stung her face and hands, pelting the blue silk blouse she had on like ice whipping her skin. The dark gray clouds of a late afternoon thunderstorm hung in the sky over the plains, lightning forked through them in a dramatic display of power that could be seen for miles. Damn. It had been sunny and cool when she went inside at noon, but she'd been forced to park the oversized dually in the street two blocks away. Stupid thing didn't fit in those little, inner-city parking garages.

Shivering, she climbed up into the cab and started the diesel engine. She should have known better. Didn't matter what time of year it was in Colorado, the weather was always a crapshoot—sunny and warm one minute, fifty degrees and stormy an hour later.

Yanking the suit jacket she'd discarded earlier from the passenger seat, she settled it around her shoulders and listened to the familiar chugging of the engine, which was a total throwback to her childhood. Every morning, she'd heard this sound outside her second-story bedroom window as her dad headed out to feed their handful of cattle and horses. Every morning at five thirty, like clockwork. The rest of the kids in school had whined about waking up to their alarms, but she'd never needed one. Seven days a week, her alarm had been a diesel engine.

Reliable. Predictable. Stable. Just like Jake.

And Jake would be an amazing father and a loving and protective husband. She didn't doubt him, not for a second. Hell, if that were all she wanted, she'd be married to him already.

If she could have both lives, she would. But facts were facts. And the biggest lie in the world was that a person could have it all. Ask any woman over the age of twenty, and they would tell you that was a big lie. Twenty-four hours in a day. Period. Unless scientists invented a transporter and something that would freeze time, having it all was impossible.

Trying to have it all would make any woman lose her mind. Kids. No kids. Married. Single. Career. Motherhood. Too many choices.

Claire took out her phone and called Emily. Her friend should be getting home today from the dig. Two rings and her friend's tired but happy voice sounded on Claire's speaker.

"Hey, Claire."

"Hey. Are you home?"

"For ten beautiful hours. I'm still trying to figure out when I can go to sleep without completely screwing up my biological clock. How's your dad?"

Claire smiled. "He's doing well. His

surgery went well and he should go home in a few days."

"Thank God. I'm glad. How is it being back? Is Mr. Hottie Cowboy still around? Have you seen him?"

Holy shit. Had she told Emily about Jake? She must have. Maybe she'd had too much tequila during one of their margarita nights and spilled the whole tragic tale. "He's still here. And actually, we're kind of hooking up."

"Oh, my God. You work fast." Her friend yawned and Claire felt the pull of sleep from a thousand miles away.

"It's not like that. It was his idea."

"Umm hmm. Right." Claire heard the pop of an aluminum soda can on the other end of the call.

"Root beer?"

"Mountain Dew. I need caffeine. If I can't stay awake another six hours, minimum, I'm screwed." Emily steered clear of caffeine most of the time, drinking herbal tea and seltzer water, both things Claire thought tasted like stagnant pond water. Coffee. That was her travel god.

Jet lag sucked. No question. And they had both learned the hard way that the best way to beat it was to stay awake that first day for as long as humanly possible. "Listen. It's no big deal with Jake. Seriously. It's just for two weeks. A friends with benefits deal."

Emily had the nerve to laugh at her. "And I thought you were smart."

"What's that supposed to mean?"

"You guys have history. That makes it a big deal. Me, on the beach in Cancun hooking up with a hot surfer I'll never see again? No big deal. You, with your true love from high school? The one guy you never got over? Big freaking deal."

"Shut up."

"Don't say I didn't warn you."

"Whatever. How did the last few days go in Brazil? How much did we get?"

"It was awesome. You should have seen it. We had seven tables full of artifacts. Almost two hundred. *Senhor* Gomes was thrilled, and his people have agreed to give us two years on loan for clean up and display before we have to send it back."

Claire bounced up and down in her seat. Two hundred? That was her best dig yet. "Did you pack my pot?"

Emily laughed. "Don't worry, your precious little pot is on its way to SoCal right now in the temperature controlled interior of a 747 with Doctor Pierson and, knowing him, an armed escort toting automatic weapons."

Claire tried to imagine the super-serious professor sitting inside an airplane surrounded by plastic crates and soldiers with machine guns. Emily was right, the image was comical. "He's not so bad. He called in a favor and got me an interview at the museum here in Denver."

"Bitch, no. You can't be serious. You can't leave me."

"I'm not. I already know I'm going to turn it down. But you should see the stuff they've got from Pompeii."

"No, Claire. Don't you start with that Italy bullshit again. We gave it a shot, and got nothing. We're going to Mexico, woman. Or Egypt. Italy is not on the radar." Emily took a very loud sip of her soda just to irritate Claire. "No sexy Italian men. Not an option."

"Yeah, yeah. I know." Claire grinned. They'd worked on their grant proposals together, made a list of the best sites, those most likely to be approved because they hadn't been fully explored. This time around, they'd settled on a remote site in Egypt and one in a little known Aztec village in Mexico. Pompeii had been a dig site for more than two hundred and fifty years. Still... "All right. I just wanted to check in. I'll be back in a couple of weeks. By then, we should have heard back on the Aztec dig."

"On both of them. And don't worry. I'll only let the stray alley cats piss in your bed every other night." Emily laughed but Claire wasn't worried. Her roommate was a very neat and orderly person. They were both gone so much they didn't have any pets, not even fish. Besides, Emily was allergic to cats.

"See you, Em." Claire hung up and turned on her GPS so she could search for an alternate route out of downtown. Too many narrow, one-way streets. And with late-afternoon traffic, she was doomed to spending more time than she was going to like in the cab of this truck.

Claire eased into traffic and decided to stop sulking. Right now, she had the world at her fingertips. She wanted to crawl in every cave, taste every exotic food, travel the world and meet people from new cultures. She wanted to live life, not sacrifice everything to keep a man.

But then again, Jake was one hell of a man.

"Shut up, Claire. Just, shut up." She cranked up the radio to distract her head from talking her in circles again. She was tired and hungry and still had to drop off some stuff for her mom at the hospital. Her dad had been moved to a rehab wing and would be home in a little over a week. And a week after that?

She'd be gone.

<><><>

The drive to the hospital took twenty minutes, and ten minutes after that she pulled the small, upright suitcase behind her into her dad's new private room complete with a whirlpool bath, a rocking recliner like the one he sat in to watch football at home, and art prints of galloping horses on the wall.

Her mom, looking worn out but

happy, was reading a book in the recliner, which also doubled as her mother's pull-out mattress. Her dad was snoring softly in his bed. Claire leaned over and gave her mom a kiss on the cheek.

"Hi, Mom."

"Hi, honey."

The old, childhood nickname made her grin. "How's he doing?"

Her mom was wearing soft pants and a cream-colored sweater, but her leather shoes were by the door. Two pink elephant slippers covered her small feet. Claire had a matching pair in her apartment. She wore them whenever she was feeling homesick. Her mom had sent them to her for Christmas two years ago. "Cute slippers."

"Thank you. You look nice, dear. How did the interview go?" Her mom placed a bookmark in the giant historical novel she was reading and set it on top of her dad's adjustable hospital table, right next to a half-drunk water bottle and an unopened, round container of melting green gelatin. Yuck. Better room, same horrible food.

Claire pulled the hard plastic

visitor's chair over from the opposite side of the bed and settled it next to her mom's chair. "It was fine. I told you, it was just a formality."

"Hmm." Her mom tilted her head to the side and Claire squirmed a bit under the close scrutiny. Psychic hotline, here she comes. "So, no chance that you would consider taking the job and moving back home."

Claire sighed, and as the breath left her body it drained all the fight out of her, clear down to her toes, which were still hurting from her earlier two-block trek in these ridiculous high heels. "No. I told you, they don't offer any fieldwork. Nothing. I'd spend the rest of my life rotting in their basement, cataloging things that *other* people got to find."

"Okay."

"I want to stay where I am, Mom. If my grant is approved, I'm leaving for eight weeks in April for an Aztec dig in southern Mexico."

"Okay."

"Okay? That's it?" Claire slumped back in her chair and studied her mom's face. Her mother had aged well. She'd be fifty on her next birthday, but her skin was smooth and the only signs of her age were the streaks of gray in her blonde hair and the laugh lines around her hazel eyes and mouth.

"That's it." Her mom reached over and grabbed Claire's hand, twining their fingers together in a soft show of love and acceptance that brought tears to Claire's eyes. After the earful her mom had given her a few days ago in the cafeteria, Claire was shocked.

"No arguments? No what ifs? No questions about Jake, or when I'm going to settle down and give you grandbabies?"

Her mom chuckled and squeezed Claire's hand. "No. I'm done judging your choices. I told your dad about our conversation in the cafeteria. And, as he pointed out, we raised you to be an independent thinker. All I ever wanted was for you to be happy and strong enough to stand on your own two feet. And you are. So, go me. Job well done."

Claire grinned. Her mom's praise warmed her heart and lifted her spirits. "Thanks, Mom."

"You're welcome, honey."

"What am I? Chopped liver?" Her dad's grumble from the bed made both women laugh.

"Yes. Everyone knows the woman does all of the work." Her mom's eyes twinkled with mischief as she answered her husband.

"And takes all the credit." Her dad chuckled, obviously still very much in love with his wife. When his warm brown eyes turned to Claire, she melted, relieved to see him looking so good, so alert. The last few times she'd been in this room, her dad had looked worn out and in pain. It was hard to see a man that was usually so vital and strong, weak with pain, his eyes glazed and dim from all the medication in his system.

"You look good, Dad."

"Damn right I do." Her dad held out his hand and motioned her over. "Where's my hug, baby girl? Just don't squeeze the ribs."

Claire went to him and leaned over the bed to wrap her arms around him. "I'm glad you're feeling better."

"I'm fine. You're the one I'm worried about. What are you going to do?" He squeezed her, tight, and his arms were like steel bands. Strong and faithful, and filled with unconditional love, just like Jake's.

"I told Dr. Levinson that I'd think about it, but I'm not ready to give up field work." Claire pulled back and ruffled his salt-and-pepper hair. That dark hair, those dark eyes…she saw them every time she looked in the mirror.

"Yes, I heard." He looked up at her and his smile was sad, "but I was talking about Jake. You love him. And that boy loves you. He's loved you his whole life."

She shook her head. "I know, but we don't want the same things. We don't want the same life."

Her dad snorted. "Life is short, Claire. And then you die. No do-overs."

"I know. Why would you tell me that?" She loved her parents, but some days, they were just weird.

"Just be sure that whatever you decide, you have no regrets. Don't leave anything on the table. You can't come back for seconds."

Claire had no idea what to say to

that, but she was saved from coming up with a response by Mitchell Walker. Jake's brother knocked on the door and stepped in wearing his usual doctor's garb. She had to admit, he looked hot. He was probably breaking hearts all over the place, because if there was one thing that hadn't changed, it was Mitchell's love of the chase. In high school, he'd been wild. After? After Mitchell's graduation, when the oldest Walker brother, Derek, took the fall for Mitchell's stupid boyhood prank, Derek had gone to jail for a few months, and Mitchell had gone from a fun-loving skirt chaser to a dark, brooding playboy who rarely spent more than a couple of weeks warming any woman's bed. The stories Jake had told her when they were still in school had made her want to kick Mitchell in the balls on behalf of women everywhere.

Looking into Dr. Mitchell Walker's eyes, Claire recognized those same shadows that had haunted a young man's eyes seven years ago. Just one more thing that hadn't changed since she'd left.

"How are you feeling, Mr. Miller?"

Mitchell chatted with them all for a few minutes, and her mother invited all of the Walker boys over for dinner as soon as her dad came home from the hospital. No, her mother didn't invite them, she demanded their presence as a thank-you for taking care of her dad's horses.

Mitchell smiled, winked at her, and said they would all be there.

Great. Just what she needed, all the Walker boys in one room.

And Jake in her house. Maybe he'd even find his way up to her bedroom.

Yep. Just like old times.

Chapter Nine

Jake patted Widowmaker's nose and led the horse to the small stream that lined the west side of his property. Crusted layers of ice lined the banks where the slower-moving water had time to freeze, but the middle flowed fast and cold, and it wouldn't freeze over again for a few more months. There weren't a lot of trees out here, but Sandbeach Lake with its white sand, tall pines, and smooth-as-glass beauty of the water reflecting everything around it including the bright blue sky, looked like an advertisement from a travel guide. This place had been his sanctuary since he was a boy. And bringing Claire here again felt like a time warp. They'd ridden the trail dozens of times before. They'd picnicked on the sand and skinny-dipped in the freezing-cold water. Having her here almost made him forget seven years of missing her.

She climbed down out of Starlight's saddle and walked the mare over to the water to join them. "It hasn't changed at all."

"No. That's one of the reasons I love it here." Jake couldn't keep his eyes off her bright pink cheeks or the sparkle in her eyes. She obviously enjoyed riding, and had fond memories of their secret hideaway.

He took his time, enjoying the fresh air and the company, and looked around. A thick forest of pine covered the sloping hills leading up from the lake's shores. Thousand-year-old limber pine grew next to bristlecone pine, lodgepole pine, and ponderosa pine. The trees were so thick he couldn't see the chunks of rock that made up the ground anywhere but along the edges of the ridges hundreds of feet away. They were up over eight thousand feet here with the timberline clearly visible, the bare peaks of the two closest mountains hovering north and west of them like sentinels guarding their private domain. The beetle kill wasn't bad here, with only a few dead, gray pine trees sticking out like sore thumbs in the otherwise green sea of color. Around the edges of the lake and along the trail, wildflowers and white Lady Tresses lined their path in welcome.

Lady Tresses were his mom's favorite flower. He always thought they looked like a tall green rope that happened to sprout some white flowers. He used to pick handfuls of them and bring them home to her, where she would fuss and ruffle his hair, and put the already wilting orchids in the center of the kitchen table like they were the most beautiful things she'd ever seen. His brothers had given him hell, of course. But Jake didn't care. He was just as tough as his brothers in his own way. He just wasn't as fucking loud as they were, and he didn't need to hear himself talk shit about it either.

He walked to the edge of the water and pulled a long green stem free. Its top was laden with about eight small white blooms. He lifted it to his nose to enjoy the sweet smell of vanilla and jasmine before handing it to Claire. His mother had even asked for blooms for her room, when she'd lay sick and dying. And he'd come here, to this very spot, to pick them for her.

Claire took the flower and lifted it to his nose. What the hell was he doing standing at the lake sniffing flowers like a girl?

Damn, but Claire was fucking with his man mojo. If Derek or Mitchell were here, they'd post this shit on Instagram and he'd never hear the end of it. But Chance? Hell, Chance would probably pick a dozen, run home, get Erin naked and rub the petals all over her skin.

It was what Jake used to fantasize about doing to Claire.

This was why he loved Colorado. Even in June, snow lined the edges of the lake and the mountaintops were white. The land could be dotted with snow and orchids at the same time.

Jake let the horses drink, then took the reins from Claire and tied both to a stiff branch on the edge of the small grove. The horses had been running for an hour, and they were ready for a break. And he was ready for some Claire.

Claire watched him with curiosity

as he opened his saddlebags and pulled out a thick blanket, two plastic mugs and a thermos. "Here. Help me out."

He held out the mugs and she wrapped her hands around them the best she could through her gloves. "I got it." He doubted the gloves would come off. Even in June it was cold at this altitude.

Jake nodded and took a few steps to their old spot at the base of an ancient limber pine and spread the blanket on the ground. He sat, leaning his back against the tree, legs spread wide enough for her to take up the space between them. He patted the ground between his thighs. "Come here."

"Just like old times." Claire's gaze looked excited, but also sad, and he understood the mixed emotions all too well.

"Not exactly." He held up the thermos. "Coffee, not hot chocolate."

"Wow. You're a wild man."

"I would be, if you'd get over here."

Claire laughed and the sound made his heart squeeze in his chest. She settled on the ground between his legs and leaned back in his arms. He handed her the thermos and she took her time pouring them each a cup of coffee. She handed his over first, and he sipped at the sweet liquid. He'd added the sugar to the thermos for her. He didn't care for sweet coffee, but his sacrifice was worth it when she took a sip of her own cup and groaned in delight.

"God, that's good."

"You're welcome, but you can call me Jake."

Claire reached over with her glove and smacked his thigh. He grinned and finished off his coffee so he could set the empty cup aside and focus on her.

Content to hold her, he let her sip at her coffee until it was gone, then took the cup from her hands and set it down next to his. She sighed and relaxed against him. The ground was cold, even through the blanket, but he didn't care. He didn't feel the cold.

"It's freezing up here, Jake. This is crazy."

"Not as crazy as the day we came up here and you jumped into the lake naked."

"You bet me fifty bucks I wouldn't do it." She laughed at the memory and he grinned, too. It hadn't been about goading her into the freezing mountain lake, his only goal that day had been to see her naked. At thirteen, he'd been very interested in seeing Claire naked. Hell, he still was. "And then you had to borrow the money from Mitchell to pay me off."

"Yeah, and that jackass made me clean his room for three months." Jake chuckled now, memories of the chaos that used to be Mitchell's bedroom coming back to him. "Mitchell used to take chocolate from the pantry and hide it in his bottom dresser drawer. After I found it, I made him give me half."

"You never told me that. Why?"

"Mitchell is a closet chocaholic. He's worse than a girl. Mom had to give up buying it. She was afraid he was going to end up weighing three hundred pounds. Trust me, I know. For three months I had to pick up all the candy wrappers from his bedroom floor."

"Poor baby."

"It was worth it."

Claire turned her head to look up at him, and she must have seen some small hint of what he was thinking about doing to her because her breath caught in her throat right before he claimed her lips in a kiss.

She shifted a bit more, until her shoulder pressed to the center of his chest. Jake took her mouth and didn't let her up for air as he pulled his gloves off and tossed them aside, not caring where they landed. He needed his hands free.

It was payback time, time to let Claire Miller know that she wasn't the only one who'd grown up and learned a thing or two. He wanted Claire to know he could take control any time he wanted to. And right now, he wanted to make her squirm, and beg, and forget everything but him.

He'd been planning this moment for hours, fantasizing about how she would feel in his arms, imagining every little thing he wanted to do to her.

Jake lifted his left arm and wrapped it around her head and down to her arm, which he grabbed to hold her in place for his kiss, and other things. His right dropped to her waist and dove under her clothing and up to cup her breast.

"Jake..." She tore her mouth from

his and pulled against his hold on her arm. She couldn't turn, and she couldn't reach around to cover herself. Her right hand was trapped against his body, and her left held in place by his firm hold on her arm.

"Shh. Let me touch you."

Their gazes met and held and hers flooded with heat. Her breathing sped and her eyes dilated as he massaged her breast and squeezed her nipple through the fabric of her bra. Her body arched into his hand and her eyes fluttered closed. "This is crazy." Her whispered words were full of heat, and need.

"Let me." Jake slid his hand across the hot skin of her abdomen to the top of her jeans and his hard-on grew as her belly quivered under his soft touch. He waited, with his hand on the button of her jeans, for her to answer him. He needed her to know what he was about to do.

He needed her to know, and be so hot for it she couldn't think straight. He needed her out of control. He needed her to feel like he had when she'd taken him into her mouth and driven every sane thought from his head.

Claire's answer was to lift her face and kiss him. She relaxed into his arms, and he felt like a conquering hero who'd just won a very important battle.

In seconds he'd released the button and unzipped her jeans. Luckily, they weren't too tight and he had no problem sliding his palm over her soft skin to her hot, wet center.

He groaned as his fingers hit that liquid fire. She was so hot and swollen already, so wet that his fingers were coated instantly. He rubbed over her slowly, enjoying the way her breath hitched and her hips pushed forward in an attempt to get more pressure there, where she wanted it most.

But he wasn't going to let her off that easy. No, he wanted her begging for release. He teased her, tracing the opening of her core, dipping the tip of his finger inside, then gliding through her liquid heat back up to tease her again. He repeated the motion over and over until she was panting. Her kisses turned hard and urgent, as if she could demand what she wanted with her lips and tongue. She brought her left hand back to grip his thigh and her fingertips dug into his muscles to the point of pain, but he just smiled and kept going, torturing her with his touch until she tore her mouth from his and buried her face in the side of his neck. She tried to brace her right boot against the ground to get closer to him, but her left leg was bent at the knee and up, where he wanted it, keeping her body open for him.

"Jake. Please."

"Give me your mouth." He loved her lips on his neck and the hot air that slipped inside the collar of his shirt. But he wanted her kiss more.

She lifted her face and offered her lips. Jake adjusted his seat, laying her back into his embrace where he could completely cover her. He wanted her to feel completely under his control, dominated and adored. He never wanted her to doubt what he felt for her. No, he wanted her to feel it all the way to her bones.

He claimed her mouth, invading with his tongue as he finally gave her what she wanted, slipping two fingers deep inside her wet heat. She writhed with pleasure and he captured her soft cries with his mouth as he gave her no quarter, pushing her hard and fast to her peak.

Her explosion rocked them both, and she tore her mouth from his with a strangled cry that he could listen to all damned day. And still, he refused to let her recover, pushing her to another orgasm just when she thought to catch her breath.

Jake kept his fingers deep, rubbing her g-spot and clit as her core muscles went through a cycle of pulsing and squeezing that arched her back and lifted her hips from the ground. When she went limp in his arms, he softened his claim on her mouth, no longer demanding a response, but gently easing her down off the edge. His hand he kept right where he wanted it, because right now, she was his. Every fucking inch of her was his, and he wanted her to know it. Feel it.

Acknowledge his claim.

But that was his pipe dream. Two weeks. That was all he had left. So, for two weeks he'd own her—body and soul.

They kissed and he held her like he

knew she wanted to be held, like she was precious and fragile, like she mattered more to him than breathing. When she tugged at her arm, he released her, pleased that she used her new freedom to wrap her arm around his neck and pull his head down so that his lips pressed more firmly to hers.

Her kiss was a thank-you, and he accepted it without words. They didn't need words. He knew her. Every look. Every sound. Every inch of her body.

And she knew him. No one had ever known him like she did, not his brothers, his old girlfriends, not even his mother. Being with Claire again was the ultimate bliss and ultimate pain at the same time.

Two more weeks.

With a sigh, she ended their kiss and lowered her cheek to his shoulder, content to rest against him. She didn't ask him to take his hand out of her pants, but he had to relinquish his hold on heaven at some point. Reluctantly, he let her go and shifted his arms so they both wrapped around her waist.

The soft sounds of the real world drifted back to him. The horses shifted impatiently on the edge of the small clearing on the other side of the trees. The small creek bubbled and gurgled with a small but steady flow of water and a gentle breeze tickled the tops of few scattered aspen trees, making their hardy handful of stubborn leaves quiver and shake. And Claire, her subtle orange spice surrounded him and her body warmed his, his personal armor against the chill air.

He held her and she seemed content to stay in his arms. For now. He closed his eyes and rested his cheek against the top of her head. This was where he wanted to be. With Claire. Holding her. Loving her. Being everything she needed.

She sighed, and the sound was so deep and tortured that his shoulders tensed before he could ask her what was wrong.

"I love you, Jake. You do know that, right?"

"Yeah. I know." The words he most wanted to hear, but instead of making him happy, they made his eyes heat and burn and his chest ache like an elephant had just stepped on his sternum. "But it doesn't change anything, does it?"

"No." Claire pulled out of his arms and he let her go. It hurt too much to hold her now. She just *had* to say it, she had to confront things head-on. Claire had always been like that—a no-bullshit, no-drama kind of girl. It was one of the reasons he loved her. But sometimes, he really wished she could just pretend for a while.

He watched her walk toward Starlight and straighten up her clothing. Her happy glow was gone, and so was his. He got up and adjusted his junk so he could tolerate the ride back to the ranch. "I guess we should head back."

"Yeah." Claire circled back to him and grabbed the thermos and coffee mugs from the ground and he followed her to his saddle, so they could repack before heading out.

He was pissed and a little hurt, until he saw the tears in her eyes. Rage he could deal with. Spit on him and call him an asshole. Shit, throw a punch, but don't fucking cry. A woman in tears made him feel like a trout thrashing on the banks of the river. Helpless and totally screwed.

"Don't, Claire. Please." He reached for her and she flowed into his arms like water, melting against him with complete trust. Just like old times. And damn if it didn't hurt like hell.

"I'm sorry, Jake. I shouldn't have agreed to this. It's just going to hurt both of us." She shook her head and burrowed closer to his shoulder, clinging to him like her life depended on it.

"No, Claire. I wanted this. We both did. And we both knew, going in, that it was going to hurt." He tightened his hold and dropped his head to bury his nose in her hair. God, he loved the smell of her...the feel of her in his arms. "I want this. Even if it's only for two weeks, I want you in my arms."

Instead of quieting her tears, his words opened the floodgates and she sobbed like her heart was breaking. Maybe it was. His damn sure was being ripped apart.

"Look, Claire. Please, don't cry. I know we don't want the same things, but don't you dare deny us this time together. Don't think about the future. Don't think about anything. Just be with me, for as long as you can."

Her hands fisted in his shirt, clenching and unclenching around the material as if she couldn't decide what to do with them. "I wish I could be different, Jake. I wish I could be happy on the ranch. I wish I could be what you want."

"You are what I want."

"In bed, yes; but not out of it. We belong in different worlds. I wish I could change for you, but I can't."

"I know. But I'm not asking you to change. I just want to be with you. Okay?" Jake tightened his hold when she nodded, her sobs slowed and transitioned to soft sniffing as she wiped her tears against his shirt. He'd just told a lie to the woman he loved and it didn't sit well with him. Because the truth was, he *did* want her to change. He wanted her to choose him. He wanted her to choose his life, his home, and the beating heart in his chest that had loved her since the third grade. But that was a dick move, and he knew it. His mother raised him to respect women, and their choices. If Claire did stay, she'd be miserable and she'd hate him for holding her back. And he just couldn't fucking live with that.

He wasn't enough for Claire Miller, and no matter how much that fact ripped his guts out and made him feel like less of man, that was just the way things were.

"We better get back." Jake kissed her temple and let her go.

They rode back to the barn and took care of the horses in a companionable but depressing silence. When she walked to her truck, he walked next to her but he was all out of friendly banter. Her dark brown eyes held too much longing, too much sadness. He knew if he looked in a mirror, he'd see the exact same thing. He ached too much to pretend it wasn't there.

He couldn't let her go completely. Not without knowing she wouldn't vanish into thin air. "Pizza night, tomorrow. Right? You'll still come? Six o'clock?"

"That's right, you supposedly learned how to cook something other than chili from a can."

"Yes, I did, but just one thing."

She grinned. "We're both insane,

but I'll be here." She gave him a quick kiss on the cheek, climbed in the cab and drove away.

There went his plan for the rest of the day. He'd wanted to take her riding, rock her world and then bring her home, lay her down in his bed, and spend the rest of the afternoon lost in her body. But right now, that just wasn't an option for him. Even if she had agreed to it, he just wasn't in the mood. Making love to Claire right now would hurt too much.

His whole plan for the day had backfired with those three stupid words.

I love you.

Yeah. He loved her, too.

Loving her was ruining his life, but he just couldn't make himself stop.

When she was out of sight, he pulled out his phone and sent Derek a text message.

You're a dick.

Less than a minute later, Derek responded. And, typical of his oldest brother, he knew exactly what Jake was talking about, without needing to ask.

Didn't need me to tell you she was going to fuck you up. Your funeral. That's what happens when you think with your second head.

Unlike you, my dick has a genius I.Q. Obviously.

I hate this. It wasn't Derek's fault, but he needed to vent, and Derek was the one all the brothers went to when shit got critical.

Lead a horse to water…

Yeah. He knew he was stubborn, but damn. This was worse than he'd thought. When he didn't answer, Derek sent another text.

Want to get drunk? I'll bring the Jack.

No thanks. Getting wasted on Jack Daniel's Tennessee Whiskey wasn't going to help. He'd just end up curled up in a ball with his head on Derek's lap, crying like a baby. Mitchell would probably record that shit, post it online, and his bastard brothers would never let him live it down.

Then go clean up that shit-storm in mom's office.

Jake couldn't think of a good response and headed for the house. He'd get cleaned up, take a cold shower, and go see what he could do in the office. For a year now, he'd let a lot of it go. And Derek was right about his apathy causing problems. So far, Jake had missed paying a couple feed suppliers and their last two shipments of hay had been delayed. The office phone was blowing up with calls from other people he'd forgotten to pay, orders he needed to confirm, vets that needed to schedule visits with the horses he was taking care of, and he had no idea which boarders had paid him and which ones hadn't. Hell, he hadn't even sent out invoices for two months.

Time to put on his big girl panties and deal with the mess.

He might as well do something useful today. Otherwise, he'd sit and stare into space and think about Claire.

Chapter Ten

Fourth Claire sipped at her glass of white wine and laughed as Jake tied an apron around her waist with the words *Kiss the cook* in bright blue across the front. "Oh, no, big boy. I can't cook. I burn toast, Jake. You've known this fact for sixteen years."

Jake's grin was infectious as he wagged his eyebrows at her and pulled a large tray from his refrigerator. "But I need you to play with my balls."

"What?" She replayed his words in her head, thinking there must be some mistake, until he lifted the lid off the food and showed her four, perfectly round balls of dough.

"If you don't play with my balls, they won't rise, and you won't be able to eat them." He pulled her into his arms for a quick kiss that was over all too quickly and she smiled up at him, content to rest for a moment with his arms around her.

"You're so bad." She laughed, but followed him to the counter where he had a rolling pin and flour spread out and ready to go. The opposite counter was lined with small bowls of ingredients to be used for each custom-made creation. There were three different cheeses, including large chunks of creamy mozzarella, sliced pepperoni, ham, mushrooms, green basil leaves, tomatoes, olives, red and green peppers, and homemade tomato sauce. The place looked, and smelled, like an Italian restaurant. Heaven.

Jake took her through the process of pounding the dough, making it into the personal-size pizza, and selecting toppings. He was a great teacher, and she hadn't had this much fun in a long, long time. By the time they were done, she had flour on her nose and a healthy arousal from watching Jake's big, meaty hands knead and stretch the pizza dough. She knew just what that felt like, when he was kneading her ass, or stroking her breasts…

"Pick your poison." Jake cut off her train of thought, pointing at the ingredients lining the opposite counter, and they carried their pizzas over to load them up for baking.

She chose a Caprese-style pizza with mozzarella, tomatoes, basil and olive oil. He stacked his pizza with just about everything and slid them both into the oven.

They made their second pizza, set them aside, and then started cleaning up. Claire threw a mushroom at Jake's head and cackled with glee when it stuck in his blond hair. Her next shot landed a red pepper slice down the front of his button-down, plaid flannel shirt.

"You're asking for trouble." Jake dug the pepper out of his shirt and raised an eyebrow. She picked up a handful of mushrooms and held them out in warning.

"Hey, I played with your balls. You owe me one."

"I'm going to give you more than one, woman. Right after I feed you and ply you with wine." Jake charged her and ducked her mushroom blast with ease. Right on top of her, she remembered just how tall he was as he crowded her against the counter, wrapped her in his arms and claimed her lips. His kisses made her whole body tingle, but her heart ache. That was Jake...bittersweet, but totally irresistible.

When the kiss ended, he held her and she wanted to stay there forever, foreheads pressed together, breathing him in.

She let it go on for about ten seconds before her mischievous side refused to keep quiet. "So, just how many are you going to give me, Jake?"

Wait, was that her playful side, or her horny side talking?

His eyes darkened with desire and she felt his growing interest pressed to her stomach through her jeans. "How many do you think you can take?"

"How much time are you willing to devote to the cause?"

"All night." Jake tilted his head to the side to check the digital clock in the white microwave to his right. "Which gives us about fifteen hours before my first feed delivery arrives tomorrow."

He turned his head and kissed his way from her cheek to her jaw, then moved down to the cords of her neck where he nibbled his way along the boat-neck collar of her burgundy sweater. "Assuming you don't want to sleep."

"Who needs sleep?" Holy shit, she was going to go nuclear right here in his kitchen.

In a move so fast her head spun, Jake lifted her off her feet and set her on the kitchen counter right next to the mozzarella cheese at the end of their pizza assembly line. He stepped between her open legs and pulled her ass forward until their lower bodies collided and her core pulsed greedily. She wanted him again, big and hard and filling her up, just like last time.

With his strong hands massaging her ass and his mouth demanding her response, she forgot about food and wrapped her legs around his hips and thighs, locking him to her.

She had her fingers buried in his hair and his teeth nipping at her ear when a loud buzzer brought her crashing back down to reality. Jake pulled away, his massive chest heaving, his hair mussed, and his lips pink from her lipstick.

He'd never looked sexier. She licked her lips slowly, and made sure he noticed as she dragged her nails down the front of his shirt to tease his nipples through the cloth. "Jake, your pizza is burning."

"Jesus, woman. You are dangerous."

She loved that she could make him forget where he was, and she had a half-dozen flirtatious comebacks on the tip of her tongue, but they were too dangerous to be spoken aloud. *Only for you*, was right there, but she closed her mouth and unwrapped her ankles from the backs of his thighs. Those three words would just get her in trouble. One, they were true; but so was the confession he'd wrung from the very depths of her soul with his hand down her pants and his steady heartbeat in her ear. She'd been ripped apart and put back together by his touch, and by the raw need she'd felt in him. He'd ripped open all of her old wounds and when she'd opened her freaking mouth, the truth had just poured out of her like acid to burn them both.

I love you? Really? That hadn't been her best moment.

No way she was making that mistake again. So, she opted for something much, much safer. "You're not so bad yourself." She shoved at his chest and hopped down from the counter when he took a step back. "It's time for you to impress me with your culinary genius."

"One masterpiece coming up." Jake held out his hand and indicated that she should take her seat at the table where he'd set out two hunter-green plates, silverware, a stack of folded white napkins, and their half-drunk bottle of wine on top of the large oval table. She took off her cooking apron and sat in the plain oak chair with a red plaid cushion padding the seat. A minute later Jake set down two small, steaming pizzas.

"Wow. They look fantastic."

"They taste even better." Jake cut them with a large, half-moon pizza cutter and served her a slice. "I promise, you've never tasted pizza like this."

Claire just smiled at him as she took her first bite. The dough melted on her tongue, disintegrated in a burst of flavor that left the basil, tomato and cheese to swirl over her taste buds in a whirlwind. She closed her eyes in bliss and took a second bite that was just as good as the first.

She opened her eyes to find Jake watching her with intense blue eyes.

"Well? Did I lie? Or is that the best pizza you've ever tasted?"

Even if it weren't the best, she would have lied to make him happy. But the truth was, she'd never tasted anything even remotely close. "It's incredible."

He smiled and wolfed down half of his first slice in one gigantic bite.

"When did you learn to make pizza?" She had finished her first slice and started on the second. The Jake she knew could barely muddle his way through boxed mac and cheese.

"A sixty-year-old grandmother gave me a lesson in the back of her family's restaurant."

She nearly choked. "What? When did you go to Italy?"

Jake's grin faded and part of her wished she hadn't asked, because she knew where this was going. Courtney. The fiancée. Her mom had told her when Jake got engaged. Claire remembered that phone call like it was yesterday. She'd hung up the phone, eaten a half-gallon of fudge caramel ice cream, watched *Love Actually* on Netflix, and cried herself to sleep.

"I went with Courtney right after we graduated from CSU. We were there for two weeks."

"Wow. I bet it was amazing." She'd always wanted to go to Italy, especially Pompeii, and the Forum, and the Coliseum. There were so many great archeological sites in the country, so much history. She had sent in her Herculaneum proposal to Denver last year, when she'd first heard the rumors about a Pompeii exhibit coming to Colorado. That obviously hadn't worked out, but she was practically drooling just thinking about it. She could spend a year in Italy and not see everything she wanted to see. "I've always wanted to go to Italy. I'll get there, someday."

"You would absolutely love it." Jake finished off his second slice of pizza and shrugged. "It was interesting. Courtney was Catholic, so we did the whole tour of Rome, the Vatican, and all that."

"How was it?"

"Hot. Crowded. I felt like a packed sardine running through a maze and saw enough art to last three lifetimes."

Claire grinned but didn't interject. Typical Jake. Cowboys and art museums typically didn't mix, and the Vatican museum housed one of the largest art collections in the world. But Jake saw more beauty in a mountain meadow than a masterpiece by Rafael or Michelangelo.

"Then we spent a few days eating gelato and drinking limoncello on the Amalfi Coast. We took the train to Pompeii and spent the whole day melting…"

She gasped and he raised his hand with a grin as he finished his sentence, "…in ninety-degree heat. And yes, Pompeii was crazy. An entire city is just standing there, empty, and the paint is still on the walls inside some of the houses."

She didn't interrupt again, just took another sip of her wine and nodded at him to keep talking. She wanted to know everything.

"Do you have pictures?"

"We probably took five hundred."

"Oh, my God. Can I see them?" She wanted to curl up on the couch with Jake and look at everything, hear everything he could tell her. And, she wanted to see what Courtney looked like, the only other woman walking the face of the planet that had to be as stupid as Claire was for walking away from Jake Walker.

"Sure, but I only kept about fifty. Courtney took the rest."

"I've seen a lot of pictures. It looks so sad." And she'd seen a replica of the plaster body castings just yesterday, at her job interview, but she was not going to open up that can of worms.

"Yeah, but the city wasn't taken by surprise like I always thought. By the time the volcano blew, they'd evacuated most of the city. Only a small percentage died, along with the poor Roman sailors in the harbor that had been sent there to try to save them."

She shoved her plate away, fascinated. "It was horrible. Did you see the plaster casts of the bodies?"

"Yes. That was disturbing. They tried to evacuate, but they ran out of time. And it wasn't exactly a well-respected city." Jake chuckled and rose to get the oven when the buzzer went off with their second pizzas.

"Did you go to Herculaneum? Or Stabiae? Was it fantastic?"

Jake brought the pizzas to the table and moved the salt-and-pepper shakers from their central location to set the steaming food down—mushroom, olive and pepper on one, and ham, pepperoni, and tomato on the other. Jake cut them into manageable-sized pieces and she helped herself to a slice of the mushroom. Her first bite confirmed it, this was the best pizza dough, best pizza sauce she'd ever eaten.

When Jake was settled again, he took a sip of wine and resumed his story. "Yes. You should have seen the bathes. Apparently, all the rich and famous went there to have a good time."

She grinned. "Ancient Roman orgies?"

"Yeah. Looked like a good time to me."

She peeled a cooked mushroom off her slice of pizza and threw it at him, where it stuck to his right cheek. "You are full of it, Jake."

"In a little while you'll be full of me, too." His total deadpan answer made her burst out laughing. Where had this Jake come from? The boy she knew had been so serious, so compassionate and intense. He never would have cracked a joke about *that*.

"Oh, my God. You're terrible."

"Which is why you can't resist me." He raised his glass in a toast, and she raised hers. She couldn't resist him, it was true. They drank to his toast and she enjoyed a couple of minutes of watching him eat while working up the courage to ask the one thing she really wanted to know. He didn't nibble at his food like a girl, he devoured it like he devoured her...with complete focus, enjoying every bite.

"What happened? With Courtney?" Claire placed her fingertips on the stem of her wineglass and spun the glass in circles on the table. She watched the liquid wobble, because she couldn't look at him and ask this question at the same time. She'd lose her nerve. "My mom told me you got engaged. Then a little while later, you weren't."

Jake polished off his second pizza and leaned back in his chair to study her. Claire could feel his eyes on her face, but she was too big of a chicken to meet his gaze. She didn't know what he'd see in her eyes, and she didn't want him to know how badly her heart yearned for an answer. He'd loved Courtney, this mystery woman that Claire had never met; loved her enough to want to marry her. Claire's mom had met Jake's fiancée, and said that Courtney was pretty and smart, with light brown hair and blue eyes. Her mother had also reported that Courtney was a good six inches shorter than Claire—shorter, curvier, and quick to laugh.

The bottom line for Claire was Jake had asked another woman to spend the rest of her life here with him, having hot sex and making cute babies. Courtney had filled the void Claire left behind.

Jake, her Jake, had fallen in love

with someone else. And even though she'd left him behind and she wanted him to be happy, that knowledge hurt her a little bit, too.

Jake's sigh was long and deep, then he leaned forward and braced himself, arms crossed and elbows on the edge of the table.

"I met Courtney my third year, in speech class. She was a biology major, pre-vet."

Claire finally looked at him. Pre-vet? So, she wasn't just smart, she was brainiac smart. Just great. Claire told the little green monster inside her head to shut up, so she could listen to the rest.

"She was fun, and smart, and she loved animals. I thought, maybe, it could work out." He polished off the last of his wine and refilled both of their glasses, which finished the bottle. "We dated for just over a year. We were both graduating, and she applied to CSU's vet school."

Claire nodded. Any native Coloradoan knew that CSU was famous for its veterinarian program.

"She got in. Campus is only an hour drive from here, so I knew it would be tough, but I thought we could make it work. I proposed, she said yes, and we went to Italy to celebrate. And it did work...for a while."

"But?" Claire watched him, fascinated as his cheeks turned pink. What the hell? Was he blushing?

"She spent six months here, but by Christmas, she left. I heard from a mutual friend that she made it through school and is a vet now, but I never heard from her again."

"But, why did she leave? I don't understand. Was the drive too much? Did she cheat?" Because Jake cheating? Never gonna happen, she'd bet her life on it.

"No. She found something...and then she left. She said she couldn't live in a house haunted by a ghost."

"What did she find?" Claire felt confusion twist her eyebrows. "And what ghost? Your house has never been haunted."

"The ghost was you, Claire. She left because she said I'd never love her the way I loved you."

Oh, my God.

His cheeks looked flushed. And yes,

he was blushing. His cute blond-boy complexion was turning a bright pink. "I'm so sorry, Jake."

What else could she say? They were a modern-day, twisted, sick, completely FUBAR'd relationship. Jake and Claire. Claire and Jake. Forever in love, but never together. It sucked, but she couldn't change the core of who she was to try to make him happy. They'd both just end up miserable. She'd had this argument with herself at least a thousand times over the last seven years. When they were together like this, it was so easy to forget everything else. Being alone with Jake was like drinking an amnesia potion, and its effect didn't wear off until they weren't sharing air.

"I'm not sorry, Claire." He turned his head to meet her gaze, and the heat blazing in his eyes made her breath catch in her throat. "She was right. And if I'd married her, you wouldn't be here now."

"But, Jake, it's just two more weeks. She could have been your forever."

Jake stood up and took her hand, pulling her to her feet to stand before him. "I'd rather have two weeks with you."

A knife twisted in her heart and she shook her head at him. She understood completely. No matter how much walking away again was going to hurt, she wouldn't give up this time with him either. Not for anything. "This is so messed up."

"I don't care." Jake lifted his hands to frame her face and she wrapped her own fingers around his strong wrists, needing to touch him. "I don't fucking care."

Jake lowered his head and kissed her like she was the only woman in the world worth kissing, like he was so hungry for the taste of her that he'd never get enough. And the kiss hurt like a hot ember searing her heart until the only reason the tortured organ kept beating was for him. Just for him.

Always it was Jake.

His arms crushed her to him and every thought fled her. She wanted him skin to skin. She wanted him filling her up. She didn't want to think about leaving him right now, she only wanted to feel.

Chapter Eleven

They made it to his bedroom because Jake carried her there. She didn't need to look around to know that a king-sized bed dominated one wall, or that his dresser would be on her right with at least one pair of cowboy boots kicked off onto the floor next to it, and a couple of well-worn cowboy hats would be resting on top of the gnarled wood.

Lips fused, Jake kicked the door closed behind them and a thrill rushed through her as he tossed her on top of the soft tan-and-rust-colored duvet. He turned on a small bedside lamp and stood next to the bed. He held her stunned gaze as he yanked off his flannel shirt and stripped down to all his naked glory. His chest had filled out since he was a boy, the wiry strength of his youth now mouth-wateringly bulked up, with massive pecs and shoulders. The soft lamp light cast dark edges to his eyes and jaw, and gave him a dark intensity that made her pulse leap. He wasn't built like a man who spent hours in the gym. He had the sharp edges of a man who'd come by his strength naturally, through hard work and honest effort.

Claire lay on her back and propped herself up with her elbows so she could admire the view. She couldn't tear her gaze from him and he stood before her like a marble statue, content to let her look her fill. Her wandering gaze slowly drifted up from his muscular thighs to his trim hips, and over the undeniable proof that he was as turned on as she was. She studied the hard lines of his abs and chest, inspected the towering power of his tall body, and longed to taste every inch.

When her gaze finally clashed with his, the heat she saw in those ice-blue eyes could have melted a glacier.

"You done?" Jake raised an eyebrow and she knew that once she said yes, she wasn't going to get another chance to look at him, at least not for a while. And damn if that didn't make her squeeze her legs together to try to stem the ache there. She wanted him to pounce. Craved it. She wanted to be consumed by him.

"Yes."

Jake turned to his bedside table and took several condoms from the top drawer. He dropped them on the tabletop with deliberate slowness.

Four. There were four.

She shivered and looked back up at him.

He grinned and knelt on the edge of the bed with one knee. He tugged her into a sitting position and pulled her sweater off over her head, tossing it behind him to land haphazardly wherever it happened to hit the floor. Watching his hands move to the front clasp of her lacy pink bra, she forgot to breathe as he freed her breasts and slid the straps halfway down her arms. He left the silken straps there and abandoned the task to caress her firm lobes and tease her nipples, gently rolling them with his fingers.

A soft moan escaped her throat as Claire let her head fall back. She shoved into his touch, hungry for it. Hungry for him. God, he felt so good. She'd missed him so much. "Hurry, Jake."

"Oh, no. Not this time. This time, you're mine." Jake pressed her shoulders back into the bed and kissed his way from her neck, down the valley between her breasts, to the waist of her jeans, where he lingered, pressing his lips to every inch of skin along the top edge of her waistline.

Her arms were trapped by the straps of her bra, but she could bend them at the elbows. She buried trembling fingers in his blond hair and squirmed. "Jake."

"Hmm?" His tongue slipped beneath the button of her jeans to tease her and she gasped.

"Hurry."

"No."

He was going to kill her. That was it. Her panties were so wet with desire for him she could feel the cool air in the room against her core and the tops of her thighs through the dense material. She'd soaked her jeans through with lust.

She was prepared to beg, but he

knelt at her feet and took off her shoes. When he reached for the button and zipper of her jeans, she'd already unfastened them. He shook his head at her, making a tsking sound.

"Bad girl, Claire."

"I want you inside me."

Jake stared at her as he pulled her jeans down past her hips and thighs, and off. She had forgotten they existed before they hit the floor. But Jake wasn't in a hurry. He knelt over her and admired the lacy pink thong that matched her bra. His gaze darkened and Claire wiggled her arms free of the bra straps to lift her hands high over her head. Arching her back, she opened her legs wider to tease him and lifted her back up off the bed, offered her body to him without reservation. She trusted him completely. He could have anything he wanted. Anything. She was his. Always had been.

He didn't speak, just dropped to his knees at the side of the bed and pulled her toward him by her ankles, placing one over each shoulder. His gaze drifted from her peaked nipples to her melting core, where his attention lingered.

When he dropped his head to tease her with butterfly kisses along her inner thighs, she shivered and fisted the fabric of his bedding in her hands. If he didn't do something soon, she was going to beg. Seriously beg, and mean it.

Claire closed her eyes and moaned as he rubbed his calloused palms from the insides of each ankle up to her knees, along her inner thighs, until the tips of his fingers rested on each side of her aching center. The small strip of fabric covering her wasn't enough to stop him from touching, or tasting, or fucking her senseless. That was why she wore them.

Jake pulled her folds open slowly, hooking the thong with one finger to get it out of his way...and then his mouth was on her. He suckled and licked, then slid two fingers inside her to push her over the edge in a fast and furious rush that she didn't even try to fight.

Jake stroked her down from the peak, never quite letting her catch her breath before he put his mouth on her and forced her body to respond again. She never came down off the edge, never stopped shaking, couldn't think, couldn't breathe, couldn't talk, she could only feel.

She shattered again and didn't recognize the wild sound that echoed in his bedroom, the female cry was too primal, to wild to have come from her.

Jake shifted slightly, and she barely had time to realize he was sheathing himself with a condom before he stood, lifted her ankles to his shoulders and pushed forward, stretching and filling her.

"God, you're tight." His tremors registered where he held the sides of her thighs and she used her feet on his shoulders as leverage to shift her hips and take him in faster, deeper, opening herself to his invasion.

He slid home and she cried out, clamping down with her inner muscles just to enjoy the sound of his tortured moans. She knew she was swollen inside, and hot, and wet. And he felt so damn good, she knew that one more touch and she'd explode all over again.

And she wanted that, wanted to feel her core pulse and spasm around his hard length.

Reaching down, she found her left

nipple with one hand and her swollen clit with the other. She paused, waiting until he looked at her so he'd know what she was doing before stroking herself into a massive orgasm all over him.

"Holy shit, Claire. You're so fucking hot." Jake watched her every move with an intensity that should have scared her, but just made her hotter.

When she was gasping for air and coming down from her release, he released her legs, leaned over and lifted her to place her beneath him in the center of the bed. Still connected, he came down on top of her and pressed hard and deep until he bottomed out inside her. She wrapped her legs around his hips in encouragement and tugged his head to hers for a kiss.

She wanted him out of his mind.

He pumped into her like a man possessed, like he couldn't stop even if he wanted to. And she opened to him in every way, sucking on his tongue as he took her mouth with the same ferocity he was claiming the rest of her.

This was not Jake the seventeen-year-old virgin, this was Jake the man.

Jake, out of control and wild — just like she'd dreamed.

He kissed her through his orgasm, and she squirmed to take him deeper when she felt him stiffen and jerk inside her. She didn't want it to end. Not yet.

Not ever.

He stayed where he was, perched over her with most of his weight on his arms, and kissed her. Kept kissing her as the storm settled and the world once again invaded her senses. She smelled the pine scent of his furniture, the clean scent of soap and softener drifting in the air above his bedding, and him — pine and leather and man.

When she could finally breathe without shuddering, could hear something other than her own pulse pounding in her eardrums, and Jake's kisses had become slow, leisurely explorations of her mouth, Jake pulled back and rested his forehead on hers. Reluctant to come back to reality, Claire sighed and looked up to find a smiling Jake watching her with the devil himself in his eyes.

"That's one."

<><><>

Three days later, Jake stood on the front porch of Claire's house with Derek and Mitchell standing beside him, one at each shoulder, flanking him like bodyguards. They were all decked out in their Sunday best, which meant Jake was wearing a pair of pants and a button-down shirt out of respect for Mr. and Mrs. Miller. Derek had on black pants, a collared shirt and a sport coat, which made Jake wonder if he was hallucinating. He couldn't remember the last time he'd seen Derek in anything but jeans and a T-shirt. Mitchell wore a suit and tie, like he'd just come from a hospital board meeting. The outside world saw a professional and highly skilled surgeon, but all Jake saw was an eight-year-old playing dress-up in daddy's work clothes.

The Walker brothers looked presentable, but he hesitated to ring the bell. One, they were five minutes early for dinner, which his mother taught him was worse than being five minutes late. And two, Derek was scowling and

Mitchell was acting like he was a second grader busy teasing his baby brother about a cute girl on the playground. Nonstop. Except Mitchell wasn't chatting about putting worms in Claire's hair, or throwing a grasshopper onto her shirt. No, he was talking about hot, sweaty sex.

"Tug your right ear if you can't control yourself and need to take Claire upstairs." Mitchell tugged on Jake's earlobe to help illustrate the point.

"Shut up." Jake shrugged him off and sent his right elbow into Mitchell's gut for good measure. His brother grunted, but didn't relent.

"If you're going for the bathroom quickie, wink at me with your left eye, and I'll cover for you."

"Shut it, Mitchell."

Mitchell was such a pain in the ass sometimes. Ever since he'd let that idiot high school girlfriend nearly cost him a scholarship and got Derek thrown in jail, Mitchell had been one miserably unhappy, serial play toy for women. Mitchell thought he was fooling them all, but Jake knew pain when he saw it, and Mitchell's pores practically oozed with regrets.

Fucking idiot.

"If you need me to clear the room, grab your nut sac and…"

Jake ended that suggestion with another, harder elbow to Mitchell's gut. "I can't believe the world thinks you're some kind of god just because you cut people open. You're a child who can't get past third grade bathroom humor."

"This isn't a comedy, little bro. It's a fucking tragedy. Why are we here?" Derek crossed his arms and asked the same question Jake had been wondering about all day long. Why was he here? With Claire's parents? It was practically a suicide mission.

Jake shrugged. "Ask Mitchell, this is his party."

Mitchell reached over and rang the doorbell before Jake could stop him. "I visited the lovely Millers at the hospital and they invited us to dinner as a thank-you for looking after their horses…and because Mom would have whooped our asses if we said no. So we said yes."

"No, *you* said yes. This is a disaster waiting to happen." Derek crossed his arms and shook his head. "Sleep with her, Jake, fine. I get it. She's hot. But you don't visit the fucking parents. That's a whole new level of fucked up. They're going to think you're serious about her." Derek shook his head.

"Maybe I am."

Derek raised one eyebrow. "Then you're an idiot because she's not serious about you. How many times are you going to let her do this to you, man?"

"Shut up, Derek, and just let it go. Okay? I can't deal with this interrogation bullshit right now." Jake sighed and thought he heard footsteps coming toward the door just as Mitchell smacked him on the ass and wiggled both eyebrows like Groucho Marx.

"Go get her, champ."

Jesus, where was Chance when he needed him? Their older two brothers were out of control, and he needed his reasonable brother here to help level the playing field. Without Chance, he was outnumbered. But Chance was in New York with Erin, and that son of a bitch wasn't coming back until Erin's North American concert tour was over. Not that Jake could blame him. Chance was head-over-heels, out of his fucking mind, in love with his fiancée, and Jake could completely understand that reality. That was how he felt about Claire.

Except Chance got to keep his woman.

Not without sacrifice.

That strange voice had been buzzing around in his head the last couple of days. He'd spent the last three nights with Claire, making love, talking about all the places she'd visited and the things she'd done, the places she seen and all of the amazing things she'd learned. Her eyes lit up like Christmas lights when she talked about her work, and for the first time since she had left him seven years ago he was beginning to understand the truth. She loved what she did, truly loved it as much as he loved the land. It was part of her deepest self, something that made her happy, and excited, and content with her life. He understood the feeling, but couldn't quite get around the bitter fact that she couldn't do what she needed to do here, with him. She couldn't give it up and be happy, no matter how much she loved him. And she did love him.

He saw it in her eyes every damn day.

He almost wished she didn't. Maybe then this fucked-up situation would hurt less.

The bottom line was, the opportunities she needed didn't exist here. Period. Which meant Claire was leaving. Again. No doubt about that. And worse, he couldn't even think about asking her to give it up. And he couldn't leave the ranch. That land and those horses were as much a part of him as her career was part of her. He'd built the fence around the barn with his bare hands when he was fifteen. He'd hung that porch swing for his mother with his brother's help on Mother's Day when he was twelve. They'd spent three hours yelling and cussing at each other while Mrs. Miller covered for them by taking their mom shopping in town. He'd never forget the pride that had made him puff out his chest like a rooster when his mother had returned home to find her boys lined up next to it. She'd made a point to sit in that swing every day for months just to make sure they all knew how much she loved it.

Every rock and tree on the ranch

held a memory that anchored him. Every room in his house was haunted by ghosts—not just of Claire, but of his entire childhood. He barely remembered his real parents, but he would never forget the pain of losing them. When he'd arrived in that house, he'd been scared and hurting so badly he couldn't remember his own name. The quiet beauty of the land had soothed him almost as much as the love of his new family. Leaving it would be like tearing out a piece of his soul.

Kind of like losing Claire.

As Claire had said to him many times over the last few days, this was so messed up.

Mitchell batted his eyelashes and started imitating Claire, which pissed Jake off. He had a fuse about three miles long, but Mitchell, in true brotherly fashion, was about to burn his way to the end of it. The last thing Jake needed was Claire opening the door to this front porch circus, or watching Jake punch his brother in the nose—which was a real possibility because now Mitchell was blowing in his ear, whispering sexual innuendoes as if he were Claire talking dirty. Jake's right hand fisted at his side just as Derek's finger thumped Jake, hard, on the back of the head.

"Ow! What the fuck, man?" Jake turned to his left to glare down at Derek. At the same time, Jake spread his entire right palm over Mitchell's face and pushed the obnoxious little shit about three feet away from him. He would have hit Derek, too, but he had a bouquet of flowers in his hand for Mrs. Miller and he didn't want to bend the petals on the bright yellow blooms.

"Jake, just don't fool yourself. Don't let Claire rip your dick off." Derek nodded toward the door just as Claire opened it for them.

Mitchell laughed. "Don't worry, Derek. Jake's dick is titanium plated."

"Shut the fuck up." Jake snapped just as he turned to find Claire outlined in the open doorway. Had she heard that? Shit.

"Ah, the lovely Miss Miller. A pleasure to see you again." Mitchell tried his best to recover from Jake's shove and regain his balance, but he was jumping on one foot, trying to catch himself when Claire had opened the big red door.

"Mitchell." She put Mitchell in his place with a well-practiced glare that made Jake want to laugh out loud and kiss her senseless. Mitchell was obnoxious as hell when it was just the guys, but their mother never tolerated disrespect to a lady and all the Walker boys had learned well.

Claire slowly took her gaze from Mitchell to look at Derek, who nodded at her in return. "Hi, Derek. It's been a long time."

"Seven years." Not a hint of friendly in that tone, and Jake clenched his jaw in annoyance. Fucking Derek just couldn't mind his own damn business.

Claire's cheeks turned pink and Jake wanted to punch his asshole brother right there. He settled for transferring the flowers to his right hand and stepping in front of Derek to break the laser-like hold Derek had on Claire's attention. "Hi, Claire."

"Hi." Claire lifted her troubled eyes to his and the shadows left her soft brown gaze as he looked at her, willing her to think about him, not his stupid brothers, and the thousand kisses he'd used to trace every dip and curve of her gorgeous body last night.

She must have picked up on something because the soft pink of her cheeks bloomed into a full-on, bright red blush.

"Well, don't linger in the doorway, boys. Come in. Come in." Claire's father hobbled up behind Claire to stand in the foyer. His arm was in a sling, but he was up on his feet and walking around, which was a good sign. It was nothing less than what Jake expected from the stubborn old man. Mr. Miller was in his fifties, dressed in overalls with a button-down, long-sleeved blue denim shirt beneath. The older gentleman was clean-shaven, his dark was hair peppered with gray, and he was using the same dark, intelligent eyes that Claire often turned on Jake to watch every move the Walker brothers made. Hell.

"You look good, Mr. Miller." Jake stepped inside and offered his hand to their old family friend.

"Thanks, Jake. I feel like an old, worn-out tractor that's missing a wheel."

"You'll get it back in no time, Mr. Miller. You're doing great." Mitchell stepped inside and shook the older man's hand like a perfect gentleman.

What a crock of horseshit. Jake wanted to thump Mitchell upside the head just for being an ass, but he could practically hear his mother yelling at them to knock it off already and mind their manners. Still, Jake couldn't wait for a woman to come along and put Mitchell in his place—preferably on his knees, begging for mercy.

"Mr. Miller." Derek stepped around him and Claire to shake their host's hand and Mitchell closed the door behind them all, trapping them in the house.

Jake just prayed nothing truly horrifying happened before he could run his brothers out of the Millers' house.

Chapter Twelve

Jake and his brothers followed Claire down the hallway to the dining room, where Mrs. Miller stood waiting with a smile on her face and a giant bowl of dinner salad in her hands.

"Welcome, boys! I'm so glad you could make it. And I'm so sorry about your mom." Mrs. Miller's words weren't necessary. She'd been at the funeral, crying like a baby. Jake barely remembered that day. He'd gone home and spent a week getting drunk every night with the stereo blasting, trying to cover the new silence that had descended on the house in his mother's absence.

"Thanks." Mitchell walked over and took the bowl from her hands to set it on the table. "Need help with anything?"

"Oh, no, dear. You boys just sit

down. This is my treat. Jake really helped us out." Mrs. Miller smiled and Jake felt his cheeks get hot. He didn't want or need any thanks from the Millers. They were practically family. If he'd had his way seven years ago, they would already *be* family.

They all sat, Mitchell and Derek on one side of the long oak table, Claire and Jake next to each other on the opposite side, and the Millers at either end. Jake fought back a sense of déjà vu as Mr. Miller's friendly chatter filled the dinner table for the next hour. He'd spent a lot of time here, back in the day, and it felt oddly like coming home.

Not much had changed. Mrs. Miller's kitchen was still bright yellow and decorated with rooster art. Their dinnerware was the same bright white plates with yellow daisies around the edge. The curtains were still an ugly olive green pattern that he'd always thought looked like regurgitated grass and the hardwood floors were dinged up and worn, but still gleamed as if they'd just been waxed.

There was a new, much bigger television hanging on the wall in the living room, and the old paisley-patterned couches he remembered had been replaced by a dark burgundy leather loveseat and two recliners. He could easily picture the older couple sitting there with the fireplace roaring and the Sunday game on as loud as Mrs. Miller would allow.

Mr. Miller was a die-hard football fan, and the blankets draped over the couch backs were blue and orange in support of his favorite team.

Everything was the same. And everything was different. How could he feel happy to be here, and sad to be here at the same time?

God, he hated getting older. He hated that he'd grown up. He wanted to go back to that seventeen-year-old kid that had taken all this happiness as his due and kick that naïve little fucker in the ass. He'd had it all, and he'd taken it all for granted. His mom. The Klaskys. His brothers. Claire…

"So, Jake, how is my boy doing out there at the ranch? He bit anyone yet?" Mr. Miller grinned like the idea was exciting.

"No. Widowmaker has been a

perfect gentleman."

"That's because Jake won't let anyone else ride him." Claire tapped her fingers next to her empty plate and grinned. "I think he's trying to win that horse over to the dark side."

Mr. Miller laughed. "That horse was born on the dark side, honey. He's hell on four legs."

"You should sell him, Dad."

Mr. Miller frowned at Claire for that. "Why would I do that?"

"A week in the hospital, Dad. That's why." Claire tilted her head as if she were the only sane person sitting at the table.

"Wasn't his fault, Claire-bear. Horses get spooked. You know that. We just had a bad day. I should've been paying more attention lead-lining that mare."

Claire crossed her arms and leaned back in her seat, obviously not too happy with her father's defense of the horse. Jake felt like he needed to jump in. Mr. Miller was right. Widowmaker was a good horse. He wasn't mean or stupid, just high spirited.

"Widowmaker's not that bad. He's

Alone With You

got a better temperament than Derek." Jake looked at his oldest brother to make sure he got his point across. Derek just shrugged.

"That's because he doesn't have three idiot younger brothers driving him crazy."

Mitchell sipped his iced tea and threw his napkin on top of his plate to start clearing dishes. "And on that note, I think I'll help you with clean up, Mrs. Miller, before I give in to the urge and punch Derek in the nose."

"Try it."

Mrs. Miller's laughter filled the kitchen and Claire's happy grin soon followed. "Oh, I've missed all you boys. So good to see that nothing's changed."

Claire was quick to jump on that. "They're all still obnoxious?"

"Adorable. All of you." Mrs. Miller nodded at Mitchell and stood to start clearing. "Makes me miss your mom even more. She would be so proud."

"Thanks, but you just sit down and let us take care of the dishes." Jake answered for his brothers and they all stood to help clear the table. He could practically hear his mom's approving chuckle.

They made quick work of the dishes, and when Claire got up to help, Jake shoved her back down with a firm hand on her shoulder. "Sit."

"But."

"Sit." Jake winked at her but looked across the table to catch Derek's angry scowl shooting in Claire's direction. "Derek." One word. That was the only warning he was going to give his brother. One word.

Derek raised his empty glass in salute before gathering up as many dishes as he could carry, which was a considerable number of stacked plates and serving dishes. He'd worked his way through college at bars and diner dives. He could probably carry the entire contents of the table to the kitchen in just a couple trips.

Derek set his dishes in the sink and went back for more. Mitchell was humming in the kitchen when Jake set his own stack of dishes down in the sink. They loaded the dishwasher together and had the whole job done in under five minutes flat. Another lesson learned from their mother.

Jake walked back out to the dining area to find Mr. and Mrs. Miller laughing at something charming Mitchell was saying. He glanced around the room, looking for the one person he cared about finding, but Claire was nowhere to be seen.

And neither was Derek.

Shit.

<><><>

Claire hummed to herself as she dried her hands on the towel and checked her makeup in the bathroom's vanity mirror. She finger combed her hair and made sure she didn't have dark smudges of black mascara beneath her eyes. When she was sure she was in the clear, she opened the door to find Derek waiting for her in the hallway. He was leaning against the wall, facing the doorway like he'd been there a while.

She froze like a deer in the headlights.

No, not headlights. Crosshairs. Derek obviously had something to say to her, and judging by the scowl on his face, his crossed arms and the dark, brooding anger flowing off him in waves, it wasn't going to be pleasant.

"Derek."

"Claire."

She stared at him, chin up, and refused to budge or speak again until he told her what the hell he wanted. After a minute he sighed. "Look, Claire, I need you to lay off Jake."

"What?" Claire's blood started to heat, but for the first time in days the fire rising to choke her wasn't lust, but anger.

"You heard me. Stop sleeping with him."

Dozens of possible responses flirted with her tongue, but she ended up going for the obvious, and most important one. "Why?"

Derek stood up and away from the wall, and Claire didn't fail to notice that Jake wasn't the only Walker brother who had grown up while she was gone. Derek was intense with his longer dark hair and sexy vibe, and he was going to rip some poor girl's heart to shreds. Luckily, he was practically her brother, and that made her immune to his hotness, but also more vulnerable to his

Alone With You

words. "Because you're hurting him, Claire. And that's a bitch move. You already left him behind once. Don't do this to him again."

"I didn't start this. It was his idea."

"No, it was Mitchell's. And I tried to warn him off you, but as usual, he just won't fucking listen. So, you're going to have to end it. Just like you did last time. Walk away and stop messing with his head."

"I'm not messing with his head."

"No?"

"No."

"You going to stick around this time and play house?" When she didn't answer Derek glared down at her. "That's what I thought. And if you don't think this is fucked up, Claire, check the top drawer of baby brother's dresser next time you are in his bedroom. Then tell me you aren't being selfish. Tell me you aren't fucking with Jake's head."

"I'm not. That's not..." Shit. She felt the gathering tears begin to burn the backs of her eyelids and she looked down and away, unable to confront the absolute conviction she saw in Derek's dark eyes, the firm belief that what she and Jake were doing was so very wrong. "I'm sorry, Derek. I never wanted to hurt him."

Claire wiped one stray tear from her right cheek and glanced back up at Derek to find him shaking his head, his shoulders less tight and slightly slumped. "Shit. Mitchell was right. You're in love with him."

She laughed, but the sound was pathetic, not happy. "Since third grade."

"Jesus Christ. What the hell is wrong with you?"

"Excuse me?"

Derek lifted his hands to rest on her shoulders and looked right into her eyes. "You love him. He loves you. What's your problem?"

Claire nearly choked as she whispered the truth to one of the only people on the planet that knew Jake at least as well as she did, his brother. "He wants a country girl, Derek, a baby-making housewife that will sit with him on the front porch so they can grow old together. And that's not me."

"You don't like the idea of kids, or the porch swing?"

Claire shrugged. "I don't mind

either of those things, but they're not enough for me. My career is important to me, Derek. I can't give it up. And Jake won't give up the ranch. So we're just stuck in two different worlds. We both know the score. Nothing's changed."

He tilted his head to the side and studied her, but didn't disagree with her assessment and that, in a weird way, confirmed the truth. The pragmatic acceptance in Derek's eyes made her heart crack open even wider than it was before. "Then end it, Claire."

"I don't have to. I'll be gone in a week."

He let her go, shaking his head. "No you won't. No, you fucking won't. You'll be here for years."

"What?" Claire was about to ask for clarification when Jake appeared at the end of the hallway. She jumped in alarm and stepped back from Derek, realizing now how close together their heads had been while talking, like two best friends sharing secrets.

"Hey, Claire. You okay?"

"She's fine, cowboy. We were just having a talk about porch swings and grade school. A little trip down memory lane." Derek walked to Jake, slapped him on the shoulder and shoved past him, heading back toward the dining room. Claire heard him ask Mitchell if he was ready to take off.

A couple minutes later, she heard her mother's goodbye and the front door slam. Through it all, Jake stood at the end of the hallway watching her.

She swallowed her anger and confusion into a tight ball that rested just above her gut and walked toward Jake. He opened his arms and she walked into them right there in her mother's hallway. Her parents knew the score. She'd confessed everything to both of them right away. She wasn't twelve anymore, but her parents still wanted to know where she'd been sleeping at night and Claire had no reason to lie.

"You okay? Was Derek an asshole?"

She closed her eyes and pressed her cheek tightly to his chest so she could listen to his heart beating in her ear. "No. He was fine. He's just worried about you."

Jake's arms tightened in a quick squeeze as he protested. "He should mind his own damn business."

Claire chuckled. "Right, because that's totally his style."

"Exactly." Jake rubbed her back for a minute and she enjoyed his warmth and strength and just being close to him. Being with him like this made her feel cherished and safe and utterly and completely content. If she could live her entire life in this moment, she'd be fine. But the universe had to ruin everything by making another twenty-three hours and change in each day. Being in Jake's arms was heaven...it was the rest of life that caused their problems.

Jake kissed her softly, first her lips, then her cheek. "I'm heading out, too. You want to come home with me?"

Did birds fly? "Yes."

Jake grinned down at her. "Good, because Mitchell drove and I need a ride."

"You squeezed into the backseat of the tiny little sports car?"

Jake's grin turned to a full smile. "Hell no, I made Derek ride in back. He's smaller than I am."

Derek was just above average height, but he wasn't small. Claire could just see the heavily muscled Derek with his knees bent up to his chest in the tiny backseat of Mitchell's cherry-red car. Good. That bossy jerk deserved it. "Come on. I'll grab my backpack and let my parents know we're leaving."

Jake tugged on her hand to hold her in place when she tried to walk past him. "You told your parents?"

Claire stopped and looked up to find that adorable shade of pink on Jake's cheeks again. Her sexy cowboy sure did get embarrassed easily. And that fair skin of his made it impossible for him to hide it from her. "Well, I didn't want them to think I was dead in a ditch. So, yeah, I told them after the first night."

"Shit. They probably hate me." Jake let go of her to rub his hand over his face. "Your dad…"

"Knows that it's my choice." Claire tugged on his elbow. "Come on. It's fine. I'm a big girl."

Claire grabbed her things and drove the short distance to Jake's house in her dad's big diesel truck. She parked in front, like always, like she owned the place, and sat for a minute with the headlights on. The chill morning weather had turned to a fairy light dusting of summer snow. At this altitude, it was rare for snow in early June, but not unheard of. Claire felt like it was a special gift, just for her. The soft powder drifted in front of the truck's headlights like tiny dancing sparklers, disappearing the moment it made contact with the ground.

"I missed the snow." She turned in the seat to find Jake watching her, and smiled. "Who knew? Right?"

Claire turned back to the front as Jake got out of the truck and walked around to her side. He pulled the driver's door open. "Leave the lights on."

"Why?"

"May I?" Jake bowed slightly at the waist and held out his hand.

"Okay." Claire put her hand in his and let him help her down as she stepped off the running board and into his arms. "What are we doing?"

"Dancing."

"There's no music. And it's snowing."

Jake just grinned and twirled her

around until she stood directly in the beams of light from the truck's headlights. Snowflakes twinkled in the air all around them like silver glitter being sprinkled on them from the clouds. There he stopped her twirling and pulled her close, swaying softly as he sang to her in his deep, sexy voice.

> *When I'm alone with you*
> *Don't touch me baby*
> *The world fades away*
> *I forget the tears I cried*
> *When I'm alone with you*
>
> *When your arms are around me*
> *When you kiss my lips*
> *You take me over and*
> *I lose myself in bliss*
> *When I'm alone with you*

She recognized the song, *Alone With You*, from the radio station her mom listened to and leaned back in his embrace, lifting her face to the sky so the tiny snowflakes could land on her cheeks and hair, and kiss her eyelashes with minute glimmers of brilliance. It was cold, and wet, and so romantic Claire thought her heart was going to explode right out of her chest.

Jake finished the song and lowered her into a deep dip over his knee before kissing her, both of them with ice-cold lips and cheeks.

When she couldn't control the shivering in her legs Jake finally let her go. "We better get inside and warm you up."

She stood in a daze, waiting for him as he went back to the truck to grab her bag and get the keys. In no time, he had her inside the house and was tugging her coat off her shoulders. When they were warmed up with some hot coffee and a bag of chocolate candy that he'd bought just for her, they headed into the living room and Jake started a fire in the fireplace while she snuggled beneath the afghan on his sofa. He joined her and they sat in companionable silence, watching the fire.

"You want to play spin the bottle again?" Claire snuggled into his side, nice and toasty warm and ready to chase all the evils of the world out of her head with a few hours of mindless pleasure. But, to her surprise, Jake declined.

"No. How about we just pretend that we spun and the bottle landed on you?"

"Okay." Claire grinned. This could be fun, too.

"Truth or dare?"

Oh, yes. A lot of fun. "Dare."

Jake's long sigh confused her until he set his coffee cup down on the table and turned to look her squarely in the eye. "I dare you to answer every single question I ask you with one hundred percent honesty, even if you think you're going to hurt my feelings."

Oh, shit.

Chapter Thirteen

A tremble started in her heart and travelled fast as lightning to her hands, where she nearly sloshed her coffee over the side of the mug. The truth? Jake wanted her to bare her soul? No hiding and no games? "Okay. But I get to ask you a question every time you ask me one."

"Deal." He took her cup from her hands and leaned back on the couch. Feet up on the coffee table, he pulled her to his side and wrapped his arm around her to keep her there. Totally wasted effort. It wasn't like she wanted to be anywhere else.

"What did Derek say to you tonight?"

She squirmed and fought the urge to roll her eyes at the reminder of Jake's pain-in-the-ass older brother. "Nothing important. He was warning me off. Told me to stop sleeping with you. He doesn't want you to get hurt."

Jake grimaced but the hand he was using to pull her close was tracing soft, warm patterns on the outside of her arm, lulling her until she felt like a drowsy kitten about to close her eyes and start purring. Jake was just plain devastating to her senses in every way possible.

She didn't think to ask a question before he asked her another one. "Do you want kids?"

"I don't know…maybe someday, if I could figure out a way to make it work. No more than two, and not anytime soon. You?" She was pretty sure she knew the answer, but a lot could change in seven years.

"I think it would be nice to have little kids running around, but I'm not in a hurry, either." Jake stared at the fire for a minute before asking his next question. "Did you mean what you said the other day? You love me?"

"You know the answer, Jake."

"Do you regret leaving?" There was seven years of hurt in his voice and she had to close her eyes to gather up the courage to answer him.

"No. I don't." She loved him, but not enough to sacrifice everything she was and everything she wanted for her life. "I told you the truth, Jake. I wanted more than ranch life. And I loved you. I was in love with you. But I also knew if I stayed I would end up bitter and angry, and that would have hurt you more. I couldn't do that to us. It wouldn't have been fair to either one of us."

"And what about now?"

Claire licked her lips. Weren't they supposed to be having hot monkey sex on the floor in front of that beautiful, romantic fireplace? This heart-to-heart, soul-baring conversation was not really what she wanted to be doing tonight. In fact, this was one of the reasons she'd avoided coming back to town for the last seven years. Exposing old wounds hurt. A lot. "Now? Nothing's changed. You know that."

"No. I don't. We're both older. We grew up, Claire. You've seen the world. You've traveled and done your digging and explored. I was kind of thinking maybe you'd be ready to think about making a change. Coming home."

"No, Jake. And this isn't fair. You promised me hot sex with no strings." Claire tried to tug away from him but he held her close until she settled back against his side.

"I know. And I thought I could pull it off. But I can't. I want you too damn much. Being with you hurts, Claire. It's driving me crazy not knowing what you want. Not knowing what you need. I can't even try to make you happy because I don't know where to start.

"Why can't you be happy here, now? What do you want from me? What would it take?" Jake rubbed his cheek against the top of her head, snagging the long dark strands of her hair in his stubble.

Claire's heart leapt at the question but her head shut the idiot organ down immediately. Once again, there was no mention of love. Oh, she had her suspicions, but in all the years she'd known Jake Walker, he'd never said those three little words to her. With this conversation, Jake was treading on very dangerous ground. She didn't have an answer for him. There *was* no answer. What she needed wasn't here. Never could be. Because it wasn't him. It had nothing to do with him. If he were the only factor in the equation, she'd have married him seven years ago and never looked back. She loved him. But just being with a man wasn't going to be enough for her. Hot sex and someone to cuddle with at night wasn't enough.

What did she need to be happy? She wasn't sure, but she'd been thinking about this nonstop since she had come back into town two weeks ago.

"Freedom. To be happy, I'd have to be free to leave. I can't give up my work, and that includes three or four months of the year on the ground, on digs in other countries." She leaned forward and tugged the afghan up to cover her chest so she didn't feel so exposed. Stupid, but it helped. "I can't be the kind of woman you deserve and be gone three or four months of the year. And what about kids? I'm supposed to pop out a baby and then take off for a six-week dig in Egypt? I just don't see how that could ever work out."

Jake sighed but didn't say anything

and she leaned her head against his shoulder. "What do you want in a woman? What would you consider the perfect woman?"

"Are you trying to get me in trouble?"

"No. I really want to know."

"What if I just said you?"

"Not letting you off that easy."

"Okay." Jake shifted his feet on the table so his left leg was on top of the right. Squirming. He was squirming. "I don't know. Smart. Funny. She would have to love to ride and like being outdoors."

"That's it?"

"Hell no. She'd have to worship the ground I walk on and cook me dinner every night—naked."

"Naked?"

"As a jaybird."

She butted his shoulder with her head. "I was being serious."

"So was I, about the naked part. I don't care that much about the cooking."

She laughed. She couldn't help it. "Now that's a lie. You can't cook. You need to marry a freaking gourmet chef."

"So, she can be naked and wear one of those funny white hats?"

"Exactly."

"That would be very sexy. I like the way you think."

Claire could just see it now, Jake would walk in from the cold and she'd be standing in his kitchen, naked but for that blue, *Kiss the cook* apron and a chef's hat, making him dinner.

No. Not me. Someone else.

Claire tried to imagine this mystery woman coming into Jake's life and realized she didn't like the idea. Not one bit. But there was nothing she could do about it. Oil and water. That was her and Jake. Oil and freaking water.

They sat quietly and Claire soaked in the moment with the soft firelight playing over them and the snow falling in glittering silence outside the windows. It was picture perfect. A fantasy come to life. And it was a lie, a temporary glimpse into the life she'd turned her back on all those years ago.

This could have been her life.

And the damnedest part? She didn't feel regret that she'd left, or anger that she was here now. She suffered the same pain she'd carried for the last seven years, felt the way she always felt when she thought about Jake…torn in two.

<><><>

Claire came awake slowly, not wanting to give up the warm comfort of being in Jake's arms. They were both naked after a night of slow, intense sex and she wasn't ready to look him in the eye. Not yet. Not when her emotions were so raw and they'd had 'the talk' last night. When she'd left seven years ago, it had been hard, but she'd known without a doubt that she was making the right decision.

Now? She knew that she couldn't give up her life, or her career, to stay with Jake, but the knowledge hurt more. Maybe because, now that she'd been out in the world, she knew the true weight—the absolute cost to both sides of her soul.

Jake stirred and she kept her eyes closed as he slid out from under the arm she had thrown over his waist. Their legs were tangled together and reluctantly she let him leave her in the warm bed. Alone.

"I'm going to take a shower."

"Okay." She snuggled under the blankets and waited as she heard the shower start, the glass doors slid open and closed. When enough time had passed, she slipped from the bed and tiptoed naked straight to Jake's dresser. Derek's taunt had been haunting her all night long. What was in Jake's drawer that was so important for her to see?

Quietly, she pulled the old pine dresser drawer open. Nothing special here, neatly folded undershirts and a couple pair of thermal underwear for working outside in the cold. But there, in the bottom right corner she saw a small black bag with roped handles. It was folded in half, and not a lot bigger than a deck of playing cards.

With a quick glance over her shoulder to the closed bathroom door, she lifted the bag from where it was nestled next to the white cotton T-shirts. Holding the small bag about chest high, she unfolded the paper and opened it from the top to find two things, a small black velvet jeweler's box and a receipt.

Shaking now, she pulled the paper from the bag first and gasped when she saw both the dollar amount and the date in plain black-and-white.

Seven years. Whatever was in the box, Jake had bought it seven years ago.

Three days before she left.

"Oh, shit." No. No. No.

Claire lifted the box into one hand and set the bag and receipt back down in the drawer. Holding her breath, she slowly opened the lid to find a stunning diamond solitaire ring nestled in the velvet.

Her engagement ring.

Except, he'd never actually asked her to marry him. Instead, she'd stood on his front porch and told him she was leaving him behind to make a new life for herself.

But why had he kept the ring all these years?

Fucking Derek. Just had to ruin this for her. He just had to force the issue, force her to see what a selfish bitch she was being by stealing this time with Jake. As she stared at the twinkling diamond, reality twisted a knife blade in her gut. She was a bitch. She'd move on, and Jake would be left behind, again, heartbroken and hurting. But damn him, he loved her enough not to push, not to ask her to stay.

Jake loved her enough to let her go.

And Derek's words had new meaning.

"...end it, Claire."

"I don't have to. I'll be gone in a week."

"No you won't. No, you fucking won't. You'll be here for years."

Tears streamed down her cheeks unchecked as she stared at the engagement ring.

Why couldn't she just be happy with Jake? Why did she have to want more? It wasn't fucking fair. She should be able to be Mrs. Betty Crocker and take what Jake could offer her.

But she couldn't. She couldn't betray her deepest self. She loved Jake, but he didn't want a woman who wasn't here, with him, living this life.

"Claire?" Jake's voice broke through the fog of tears and she turned her head to find him looking hot as hell with a pale gray towel around his waist and nothing else. Any other time she would have been eager to close the distance between them and explore, but right now, the sight of him shattered something inside her.

"Why, Jake?" She held out the ring in her palm and knew she looked pathetic standing there naked, holding out the ring, trembling and crying like a hysterical freak. "Why didn't you ever ask me? Why did you keep the ring all this time?"

"Fucking Derek. I'm going to kill him." Jake closed the distance between them, but stopped when she held up her other hand to ward him off. "Claire, listen. It's not a big deal. Just put it back and forget about it."

"Not a big deal? Not a big deal? You were going to ask me to marry you, and that's not a big deal?" She shook her head. "I don't understand you. Why? If you wanted to marry me, why didn't you ask me? Why? You could have come to California with me. You could have had horses there, Jake. We could have been together."

Jake ran his hand over his face and shook his head at least half a dozen times. "Look. I don't know, okay? You left, and I didn't want to move to California. I still don't. I love the ranch,

Claire. I didn't want to leave...and I kept hoping you'd come back." He reached for her again, but she dodged him and wiped the tears from her cheeks. "I love you, Claire. I always have. I'll never stop."

"But not enough to leave your life. Not enough to sacrifice what *you* love. Which makes you no different than me." Claire closed the lid on the ring and turned her back on him to slip the box back into the little black bag, stuff it back down into the corner where she'd found it, and gently close the dresser drawer. He risked a light touch on her shoulder, but she whirled on him. "All this time I've been beating myself up, feeling guilty...feeling like a bitch for what I did to you, for leaving you. But you did the exact same thing, Jake. You chose the ranch over me. You chose your land over us."

Claire stormed to the side of the bed where they'd dumped her clothes on the floor last night in their hurry to get naked. She yanked them on as fast as she could, while Jake stood there stunned and apparently unsure of what to say. She'd spent seven years feeling like a grade-A, selfish super-bitch, and all along, he'd been just as willing to let her go. And for the exact same reasons. And now he was throwing down an *I love you*? Why now, after all these years, when they both knew it was just going to cause more pain? Nothing had changed. Not one goddamned thing.

"This was a mistake, Jake. We both should have known better." Dressed now, she sat on the edge of the bed they'd just made love in and slammed her feet into her boots, skipping the socks. "I can't believe I ever thought this was a good idea."

"Claire."

"No." She looked up at him from the edge of the bed and stood slowly, deliberately considering her next words. She wasn't sure why she was so upset, but she was. Bracing her shoulders, she looked him in the eye and told him goodbye for that last time. She couldn't do this again and survive. "I love you, Jake. I always will, but some things just aren't meant to be."

"Claire, can't we talk about this? I'm not willing to give up."

"Are you willing to move to

California?"

"I can't, Claire. The horses—"

"Are an excuse. And even so, are you telling me you've suddenly decided you're okay with a part-time wife? With me being out of the country for weeks at a time?"

"No. But you've been so many places already, I was hoping you might be ready to settle down."

"Settle down on the ranch and start making babies? Make you dinner every night and clean your house and do your fucking paperwork?" Claire's voiced dropped to a dangerous low, the tone one she only used when she was beyond furious. But Jake kept right on pushing.

"I don't know. Maybe. What's so wrong with that?"

"I'm not your fucking mother, Jake." Claire's chest clenched to the point of pain and she knew if she didn't leave she was going to lose control, start throwing things at him. Big, gorgeous, old-fashioned idiot. "Time to grow up, asshole. Your mom is gone, but you keep this house like it's a shrine to the dead. I bet if I walked into her room I'd find all her things still out on the dresser, her clothes in the closet and her shampoo in the bathroom! And you don't want a wife, you want a mother. I'm not a replacement for your mother, Jake." She grabbed her bag and stormed past him, out the door, and out of his life. For good this time.

She was a fucking, lovesick idiot. That was what she was. Nothing had changed. Jake never changed. She was done feeling guilty, done tormenting herself with blame over leaving her poor, good-old boy back home with a broken heart. He was as much a part of the problem as she was. Square peg, round hole.

Which simply confirmed her general attitude. Love was a bitch.

Chapter Fourteen

Jake heard his front door slam and sat on the edge of the bed with his head in his hands.

What a fucking disaster. And he had no idea how to fix it. He needed help. Or someone to get drunk with. His whole life was falling apart and fucking Chance was out of town. And he didn't need Derek's hard-ass bullshit right now. He was too pissed at Derek for interfering anyway. If he saw that asshole right now, he'd probably punch him.

He texted Mitchell.

Where are you? Mitchell answered almost immediately, which was a good sign. If he were in surgery or working, sometimes he wouldn't answer for hours.

Ball and chain for 48 hours. What's up?

Ball and chain was Mitchell's code for being on call at the hospital. As a level-one trauma hospital, they kept a surgeon on the grounds 24/7, which meant Mitchell literally couldn't leave the building when he was on call. Mitchell had to stay in a tiny room with a bed covered in standard hospital bedding, a small television and a desk about the size of the one Jake had used in grade school. Real high-end accommodations.

Claire found the ring.

And?

It wasn't pretty. She's gone.

Sorry, little bro. Come down. I'll kill you with hospital food and put you out of your misery.

Be there in an hour.

Jake got dressed and drove to the hospital without seeing anything around him. He just kept replaying the sight of Claire, naked and crying, holding out that damn ring like it was a torture device he'd designed just for her.

Fucking Derek had to push, had to tell her where to look. That was the only explanation. He'd been stupid a few years back and confessed to Derek, told him where the ring was. Told him all of it. God damn it.

He texted Mitchell when he arrived and his brother was waiting for him at the west entrance looking bored and exhausted with dark stubble lining his jaw and dark circles under his eyes.

"You look like shit."

"Got called in last night after dinner."

"Oh, yeah? Something good?" Good, for Mitchell, meant gunshot wounds, stabbings or other high-risk, high-adrenaline cases.

"Yeah. Guy was bleeding out. Twenty-five-year-old rolled his truck and ruptured his spleen." Mitchell's voice held the sound of satisfaction. Jake knew his brother loved that kind of thing, especially when he cheated death for his patients.

Jake, however, didn't enjoy the blood and guts side of Mitchell's job. "That's enough. I don't want to know any more."

Mitchell walked him to the cafeteria and slumped into a corner booth as far away from everyone else as possible. The room was mostly empty with only a handful of other people sitting quietly, most sipping coffee and involved in their own problems.

"You want coffee?" Mitchell asked.

"Yeah."

"Good, bring me one, too."

Jake chuckled but took pity on his brother and fetched two cups of coffee with cream, no sugar, then sat down opposite Mitchell and waited as his brother took a long, slow sip of his beverage.

"Nectar of the gods." Mitchell set his cup down and tilted his head. "So, things went to shit, huh? That was fast. You two looked nice and cozy last night."

"Fucking Derek told her where to find the ring."

"Shit. I was wondering how she found it." Mitchell tapped his fingers on the tabletop. "And?"

"And she was standing there holding it out and crying her fucking eyes out and I had no idea what to say. What the hell was I supposed to say?" Frustration boiled up inside him until he felt like he was going to explode with it. Where was a punching bag when he needed one?

"Oh, I don't know. 'I'm a pussy-whipped idiot who's totally in love with you and I want to marry you'?"

Jake snorted. "Yeah. Right. Like that would've done any fucking good at all."

Mitchell leaned forward and his green eyes were dark and intense, and way too serious. "How do you know? Have you ever tried it?"

"I told her I loved her." Suddenly Jake felt like squirming in his seat. Maybe coming to talk to Mitchell wasn't such a good idea. Maybe he should have stayed home and drowned his sorrows in a fifth of whiskey. Except drinking made him think about Claire more, not less. Which was totally messed up.

"And?"

"And what?"

"Jesus Christ, Jake. And? What did she say?"

"She said I wanted her to cook and clean and do paperwork."

Mitchell choked on his coffee and nearly sprayed Jake with the contents of his mouth. "Fuck me. Holy shit, brother. She's got you all figured out."

"What's that supposed to mean?"

"It means she's right. You love her.

You want to fuck her brains out. But you don't want her life, you want yours." Mitchell shrugged. "So, she's right. I guess you should call it good and walk before it gets worse."

"It can't *get* worse. She said that I didn't want a wife, I wanted a mother. And she gave me shit for not moving mom's stuff out of her room."

Mitchell laughed, and Jake was ready to jump the fucking table and punch the asshole in the jaw, hard. But then some poor family would get in a car accident and die because the only surgeon in the hospital who could save them, his idiot brother, was unconscious on the floor.

"Jake, we've been telling you to do that for months. It's like a shrine in there. The whole fucking house. Even the office. I can't stand to walk in there, it's like Mom's going to walk around the corner at any moment. You're hanging on to a ghost. You need to let go and move on. It's your house now. We all loved her. We all miss her. But, she's never coming back."

"I know. I just like things the way they are. It's comfortable."

"No. It's sad. It's pathetic and slightly disturbing." Mitchell finished off his coffee and crushed the cup. "Listen, I'm sorry about Claire, but she's right about that. You need to take care of it. Mom's been gone for seven months. I'll call Derek. We'll come over this weekend and help you box up Mom's stuff and rearrange the furniture. Maybe we can fly Chance in, too. Okay?"

Jake didn't like it, but he knew Mitchell was right. It was time. "All right. Fine."

Mitchell grinned. "Good. One problem solved. I'm afraid I can't help you with the other one."

"You got me into this mess." Jake watched as a woman in a long blue sundress walked toward their table. "Company coming, five o'clock." Jake nodded in the woman's direction and watched with fascination as Mitchell turned to see who it was. His brother's entire body stiffened and the easy smile left his face, replaced by a pained grimace as he rose to greet her.

"Dr. Walker."

"Ms. Finley." Mitchell blinked a few

too many times and turned to Jake. "This is my baby brother, Jake."

Ms. Finley held out her hand and Jake stood, shaking it gently. The woman was gorgeous with long auburn hair and light brown eyes that looked like warm honey. She had a laptop under one arm, a messenger bag over her shoulder, and a large visitor's sticker on her chest. She was also skittish as hell around his brother.

Holy shit. Jake grinned at her with genuine warmth. Maybe Mitchell had met his match after all. "Nice to meet you."

"You, too." She released him and turned to Mitchell. "I wanted to say thanks for taking such good care of Tyler. I just went to see him. He said he might be able to get out of here and be back on tour in a few weeks."

"Thanks. Just doing my job." Mitchell's grin was forced and Ms. Finley seemed to know it.

"I'd still like to set up time for an interview." Ms. Finley pulled a phone from her bag and opened something Jake couldn't see. Probably a calendar app. "How about tomorrow morning?

Nine? I'll meet you in Tyler's room?"

"I'm on call until Monday."

"Oh. Okay. How about next Tuesday?"

"That should work." Mitchell was staring, and Jake discreetly glanced at Ms. Finley's left hand. No wedding ring.

"Excellent. I'll see you then." She nodded, entered the date into her phone, and wandered off without another word. Mitchell watched her with intense focus until she was not just out of the cafeteria, but out of sight, around a corner, and down the hall.

"What the fuck was that?" Jake couldn't wait to rub Mitchell's nose in his own shit. "You were practically drooling all over her fucking hand."

"No I wasn't."

Jake did laugh this time because his brother actually looked guilty. "Mitchell?"

"She's an entertainment reporter for *The Post*. She wants to interview me because I operated on Tyler Travis last night."

Jake's laughter died off for two reasons. One, *The Daily Post* was the most widely read online news organization in the country. And two, Tyler Travis? "The musician? He was the spleen?" Jake loved that guy's music, and the local radio stations played Tyler Travis songs practically nonstop.

Mitchell shrugged. "Yeah. He rolled his truck and they choppered him in to the ER around midnight. I wouldn't normally mention it, but it's going to be all over the fucking internet in the next few hours anyway."

"So, you operated on Tyler Travis, saved his life, and now that smoking-hot ginger wants a piece of you?" Jake sat back down and Mitchell slid into his seat across the table.

"No, she wants an exclusive interview."

"Because you took care of Travis."

"That's what she says."

"Yeah, but you want to take care of her." Jake couldn't keep the suggestive tone out of his voice, or hold back the chuckle that erupted when Mitchell fidgeted.

"Don't be stupid. I don't have time for that."

"Uh-huh. What's her name,

dickwad?"

"I don't know."

"Bullshit, Mitchell. What's her name?" Jake had to push. "If you don't tell me, I'm going to look her up online. Maybe I'll track her down on Instagram or Facebook and post pictures of you in your underwear on her wall."

Mitchell laughed. "Shut up, asshole. You wouldn't know how to post to Instagram if I gave you a private lesson. You're as bad as Mom was. I'm not scared. You can barely work your fucking phone." Mitchell glanced back over his shoulder as if he needed to be absolutely certain she was totally, completely out of his sight. When he turned back around, Jake's grin had turned into a full smile. "Her name's Jessica."

The hospital PA system paged Dr. Walker to the emergency room and Jake raised his eyebrows.

"Duty calls."

"Saved by the bell, Dr. Walker." Jake did his best to imitate Jessica Finley's soft, feminine voice. "What were you saying about being pussy-whipped?"

Mitchell made a crude hand gesture and left Jake sitting alone with his coffee, and no answers. He still had no idea what the fuck he was going to do about Claire.

<><><>

Claire finished packing her carryon bag and turned when her mother knocked on the frame of her bedroom door.

"Ready to go?"

"Yes." Claire checked her phone, "but my flight doesn't leave for four hours, so we have a little bit of time." It was at least an hour's drive to the airport. "I can take a cab, Mom. You don't have to drive me all the way over there."

"Nonsense, honey. I'll take you. You're only going for three days. And besides, that way I get to come pick you up." Her mom came into the room and wrapped Claire up in a big hug. Claire clung, hanging on for dear life. She so needed a hug right now. Her mom seemed oblivious to her inner turmoil, which was just fine. She didn't need to hash out all the gory details of her break-up with Jake. She really didn't.

Her mom squeezed hard, then let her go. "It's so exciting! I can't believe you're going to Italy."

"Nothing's official yet, Mom. That's why I have to fly to Washington, to meet with the rest of the team." The call had come yesterday morning. Claire and her dig team had worked hard last year on their study proposal for the ruins at Herculaneum, a lesser-known ruin close to Pompeii, Italy. She hadn't counted on getting that call. Not at all. In fact, she was shocked. She'd been fairly certain her proposal through the university in California would be accepted for the Aztec dig sites. But this? Italy had been a total shot in the dark.

She ate lunch with her parents, happy to see her dad getting around so well. He had ditched the shoulder sling and gone cold turkey on his pain meds; and, with his stubborn cowboy pride, he'd probably be riding again by the time she got back from the East Coast.

"You look fantastic, Dad."

"Well, you don't." Claire froze with

half of a ham-and-cheese sandwich midway between her plate and her mouth.

"What?"

"You look like hell, girl. What happened with Jake? I thought you two were getting along."

Oh, great. Now she was going to get the third degree from her dad. And why did she suddenly feel like a six-year-old? Her dad always managed to have that effect on her, no matter how old she got. "We were, Dad, but now it's over. It was only a temporary thing."

"You're in love with him."

"I know."

"Then why? What did he do? Do I need to go have a heart to heart with that boy?"

Oh, God, no. That was the last thing she needed, her dad storming the castle to yell at Jake. Claire munched on a crispy potato chip and took a sip of her iced tea. "He didn't do anything, Dad. We just don't work."

"Why?"

"Well, for starters, I live in California and he lives here."

"That's just geography, Claire-bear." His voice softened as he used her old childhood nickname.

Claire shook her head and swallowed the lump in her throat. "We just don't want the same things, Dad. He wants me to give up fieldwork and stay home like a good little wife, and I really don't want to do that. It's hopeless." She tossed the last bit of her sandwich onto her plate like a lost cause.

"Hmph." Her dad tapped the side of his head with his pointing finger. "I thought that boy was smarter than that."

"Yeah? Well, he's not. He's old-fashioned, and sweet, and apparently not for me."

"Okay, honey. Are you ready to go?" Her mom stood in the archway with her car keys in hand and Claire's luggage behind her.

Yes. Claire was more than ready to get out of this town, out of this life, and away from the constant reminders of what following her dreams had cost her.

"Sure. Let me grab my bag."

Chapter Fifteen

Two days later, Jake looked across his desk at the deeply lined face of his new accountant and felt something shift inside. Mrs. Gregory was sixty-two and had just retired from a job in the city's billing department. She was good with numbers, good with people, only needed part-time hours, and came highly recommended by Mrs. Klasky.

That was good enough for him.

He showed her the accounting software and the stacks of paperwork and left her to it with a spring in his step he hadn't felt in months. Another freaking point to Derek. Jake should have hired someone months ago. He felt like he'd just shrugged a mountain off his shoulders.

Now, if only he could get Claire to answer his calls or respond to his texts.

He knew he was blowing up her phone, but he wasn't going to stop—not until she answered him.

I'm sorry.
Claire. Please call me.
I just want to talk.
I miss you.

The silence on her end made him want to tear his hair out and pound his head into the tile floor. He couldn't take it. She'd ripped his heart out, but it had been his own fucking fault for opening his mouth in the first place.

And fuck his brother, Derek, for being right about Claire. Sleeping with her had been stupid. And as impossible as it should be, he wanted her more than he had two weeks ago. When she'd first come back in to town, she'd been like an old wound aching and stirring to life. Now she was a raw hole in his gut that constantly bled. She was leaving, again. But this time Jake knew exactly what he was losing.

He thought he'd loved her when he was a kid. And he had. But now? Now he'd realized how much she'd always been holding back. He'd seen behind the magic curtain. For the first time in his life she'd really let him in. She'd burned him up in bed, forced him to talk about his mom, yelled at him, and called him on his shit. The shy girl who'd loved him in high school had grown up into a woman who challenged him in every way possible. Seven years ago he'd been foolish enough to think he could replace her, just find another woman to love heart and soul and fucking all-in. Now he knew better. There was only one Claire.

And it didn't fucking matter. She was leaving him no matter what he did.

He stormed up the stairs to find his brothers stacking boxes in the hallway outside his mom's old room. They'd been at it for hours, sorting and organizing her personal belongings, deciding what to keep and what to give to charity. They had a stack of boxes four deep lining the hallway outside the bedroom and they'd only emptied out their mom's closet and one dresser. Her chest of drawers and nightstand drawers hadn't been touched yet.

"Holy shit. I had no idea Mom had so much stuff." Chance closed the now empty walk-in closet door behind him and used packing tape to seal up a box that held the last of their mom's shoes. Chance had flown in for the weekend, and Jake was relieved that his brother was willing to rack up the frequent flyer miles. Clearing out his mom's stuff was hard enough. Mitchell and Derek were on their best behavior, but they were still hardasses who never seemed to really get Jake the way Chance did.

"No wonder you didn't take care of this, Jake. It would have taken you a week to do this by yourself." Mitchell was wearing shorts for the first time in months and Jake barely held back the urge to make fun of the doctor's milky-white legs as Mitchell knelt on the floor and opened the bottom drawer of the chest. He had two empty boxes on the floor next to him. Derek had gone outside to back the truck up to the front door so they could start hauling stuff out.

"Yeah." Jake walked to the stripped mattress and sat down close to the nightstand. The mattress was going tomorrow, and so was his mom's bed set. He couldn't look at the bed frame or dresser without drowning in bad memories, and he knew his mom wouldn't want that. And there was no fucking way he was ever going to sleep in that bed again.

He'd spent three weeks sleeping in here, right next to the hospital bed they'd brought in for his mom when she got too weak to walk. He'd carried her to the bathroom and helped her stand up in the shower. He'd fed her when she couldn't feed herself, and read to her when her eyesight went, but the pain kept her awake.

This room had been his own personal hell on earth, and his brothers had popped in to check on them for an hour or so in the evening, or for a Saturday afternoon. But Jake was the one who'd been here, watching their mother cry and ramble and lose track of time. He'd been the one holding her hand when she was scared.

Twenty-four years old, and he'd lain awake in this bed listening to his mother's death rattle, afraid that if he left the room she'd call for him and he wouldn't hear her.

He'd lost another mother in this room, watched the coroner wheel her out on a gurney like a piece of meat under a sheet. And when everyone left, and the casseroles and cards stopped coming, it had just been Jake and the house.

And silence.

"You all right?" Chance stood with his hands on his hips, watching Jake like a hawk, and he realized he'd been sitting on his mom's bed, staring into space.

"Yeah. Just sucks, you know?"

Chance squeezed Jake's shoulder before picking up his box and carrying it out to the hall. Jake reached over to his mother's bedside table and opened the top drawer.

There, right on top and dead center was a white linen envelope with his name on it. The writing was jerky and harsh, as if his mother had struggled to write just four letters. And taped to the outside were two Lady Tresses. The stalks were shriveled, and the flowers were dried out and crumbling from their time in the drawer, but there was no doubt in Jake's mind they'd come from the lake, or that he'd brought them to her. He remembered that day, the last time she'd known who he was, before the morphine and tumors had taken her mind. She'd been gone even before she died. He'd lost her twice.

Fuck.

Shaking, he reaching into the drawer and lifted the card and flowers onto his lap. His hand trembled and his vision blurred. Derek walked back into the room, but Jake ignored his brother and used his thumb and middle finger to wipe at the moisture gathering in his eyes. He wasn't going to fucking cry. He'd done enough of that shit when she died.

"Is this what I think it is?" Mitchell pointed to the small urn sitting on his mother's dresser just as Chance walked back into the room.

"Yeah. It is." Jake wasn't going to deny it. It was a fucking urn. What else did they think it was?

Mitchell turned to Jake. "I thought you took care of this?"

Jake shuddered and stood up with the card in his hand. "I will. I just haven't gotten around to it yet."

"Jesus, Jake. You told us you took care of it at Christmas." Derek looked up from where he had crouched on the floor on the other side of the bed. He had several boxes and vacuum-sealed bags on the floor next to him that he'd dragged out from under the bed. Their mother had a gift for stuffing boxes and storage containers in every available space.

Jake shrugged but didn't answer. There wasn't much to say. The bottom line was, he just hadn't been able to force himself to spread her ashes like she'd asked. Not yet. He would get around to it, when it didn't hurt so fucking much. Which would probably be around the same time he actually opened the card...maybe when he was thirty.

He stared down at the card in his hands and ignored them all. He couldn't look at them right now. He couldn't fucking breathe. He needed to get out of here.

"We're a bunch of assholes." Derek walked straight up to Jake and wrapped his arms around his little brother. Jake tried to hold it back, but his whole fucking life was falling apart, and being back in this room, reliving all the pain of watching his mom wither and die was too damned much.

He held on to his control by a thread until Mitchell and Chance closed ranks around him and all three of his brothers wrapped him up in a circle so tight they could have held his massive ass up off the ground if his legs gave out.

That was when the tears came. For his mom. For the life he'd been forced to lead out here with her on his own after Courtney left. Alone, and dealing with death when he should have been out partying with friends and living his own life. He didn't regret those months, and he'd always hushed his mother when she'd tried to talk him into hiring a nurse and leaving her be.

But it had been hard, and it had made him bleed in a way he'd never wanted to bleed again.

He didn't remember his biological family, but he remembered the pain of losing them.

Jake's shoulders shook as his family held him up, his brothers not by blood, but by heart, and soul, and choice.

Chance's head was pressed to Jake's right temple, and his words just made it harder to breathe. "I'm sorry, Jake. God.

I'm a dick. I should have noticed how bad you were hurting." Chance's voice wavered, thick with emotion. "It was too fucking easy to leave you out here to deal with it. I couldn't stand to see Mom like that. I was weak...a fucking pussy. We were all chicken shit. It hurt too much to come out here. I'm sorry for that. You're the youngest, and we should have had your back, not left you out here alone to deal with all this shit."

Mitchell was behind him, forehead pressed to the back of his neck. "I love you, little brother, and I'm sorry, too. But this is bullshit, man. You should have said something. You should have asked for help."

Jake couldn't talk, but he shook his head. Ask for help? Help with what? Being a pussy? Missing their mother? Hating the silence? Feeling alone? He had it covered. He didn't need help with any of that shit. He was the master.

Derek's arms were wrapped around Jake's chest and sides like steel beams, and Derek wasn't letting go. His face had to be less than an inch from Mitchell's, but Jake wasn't ready to lift his head off his big brother's shoulder to look. "No, man. Chance is right. We never should have left our baby brother out here to deal with all this on his own." Derek squeezed until Jake could barely breathe. "I'm sorry. I'm so sorry. I love you, Jake. I love you, man."

The big group hug lasted another minute, until Jake sniffed and shrugged his brothers off him like a giant bear waking up from hibernation. "Get off me before our dicks fall off."

Chance burst out laughing, but let go first. Derek let go and shoved at Jake's chest with a grin. And Mitchell? That motherfucker grabbed the card out of Jake's hand and jumped across the bed before he could get it back.

"Let's open it together, shall we?"

Jake turned on him and felt his tears dry up quick. "Give it back."

"You going to read it sometime this century?" Mitchell raised his eyebrows. "Or should I read it to you while we're all here together?"

Fuck. Mitchell acted the clown, but he totally had Jake pegged. All the anger drained out of him, leaving him feeling numb. It would be better to know, but he wasn't sure he had the nerve to open the card and deal with whatever was written there on his own. "Since we all turned into a bunch of girls anyway, go ahead."

Jake sank down on the bed and scooted up so he could sit with his back pressed to the headboard. Mitchell plopped down beside him as Chance and Derek sat near the bottom. It was like they were kids again, all curled up around their mother's feet listening to a bedtime story. Except this wasn't going to be a story about pirates or cowboys. This was going to be all about goodbye.

His eyes started to burn again as Mitchell broke the seal on the envelope and pulled out a card. It was a photocard from one of those internet sites, and the picture on its front was of Jake with their mother when he was about thirteen.

"Hey, I took that picture." Chance grinned, please with himself.

"Yeah." Jake nodded and lifted his T-shirt to wipe at his cheeks again. The photo was taken on the front porch swing. He was sitting next to his mother with his head on her shoulder and they were both laughing as he held up the ridiculous sheet of printed directions they'd tried to use to put the swing together. The paper was taped down the middle where Chance had torn it in half in frustration. Mitchell had drawn faces and cartoon figures all over it, and Derek had ignored the instructions completely and said they should just figure out how to assemble it on their own. Which he had. Several hours later.

Mitchell took a deep breath and opened the card. "Jake. My son. I'm so sorry you had to be here with me while I get sick and die…" Mitchell's voice faded and he paused to wipe at his own cheek. "This is going to suck. It's printed out, and it's long."

"Just read it." Derek crossed his arms, leaned back against the footboard of the bed and stretched his legs out along Jake's. Touching. So Jake would know he wasn't alone.

"Read it." Jake closed his eyes and leaned his head all the way back against the headboard as Mitchell read aloud.

"Jake. My son. I'm so sorry you had to be here with me while I get sick and die. I never wanted this for you. My biggest regret with this cancer is that you have to suffer with me. I'm sorry. I know your shoulders are broad and you will bear the burden. I want you to know that every time I see you I am at war with myself. I have become so frail and reliant on your strength, and I hate myself for it. I should be stronger. I should force you to leave me, but I can't. I see the pain in your eyes, but I'm too scared to let you go.

"Courtney's gone. Your brothers have all moved on and are out in the world living their lives. That's what I wanted for all of you boys and there's never been a prouder mother. But I feel like you are stuck here—dying with me.

"Please forgive me, my beautiful boy. Forgive me for getting sick. Forgive me for needing you now, when things are so painful and ugly. Forgive me for instilling the same love for this land in you that I've carried all my life. It kept me here long after I should have moved on. It's not easy living out here alone. But it's too late now. I see it in your eyes when you watch the sun set, or the wind bend the trees. The mountains are in your blood, as they were in mine."

Mitchell dragged a deep,

shuddering breath into his lungs and cleared his throat. "Holy shit. This is hard."

Jake nodded. No shit. It had been hard when she'd been lying there dying, too. And this was bringing all that old pain up like a raging tornado in his chest. "Just hurry up, Mitchell. Seriously. I don't know how long I can sit here."

"Amen to that." Chance wiped at his cheeks, Derek sat silently, staring at his feet, as Mitchell cleared his throat a second time and started reading again.

"I am ready to go now, to end our shared pain. I know it won't be long before the Lord calls me home, but I couldn't go without saying thank you. Thank you for sitting with me and bringing me my favorite flowers. Thank you for reading to me on the days when your voice is the only thing that keeps me sane. Thank you for carrying me around like a broken doll and holding me up in the shower. Thanks for enduring the embarrassment of helping me in the bathroom and making me tea. Thank you for a thousand things you never should have had to do. I love you, son. I love you.

"Tell your brothers I love them. And please, be happy. Live. Love. Take risks. I have no regrets. I loved you boys with everything in me and always will.

"Thank you, son. When the sunlight hits your hair, it will be me smiling down on you from heaven.

"Love you forever.

"Mom."

The silence was heavy until Chance got up from the bed and returned a few seconds later with a box of tissues, which he passed around. They all took one.

"Holy shit." Jake dabbed at the corners of his eyes but didn't move his head. His skull pounded with a raging headache and his eyes felt heavy and sore. He was a fucking mess.

"That's it. You're officially the most badass Walker brother." Mitchell punched him in the shoulder. "I thought Mom hired a nurse, Jake. What the fuck was all that about showers and the bathroom?"

Jake shrugged. "She didn't want a stranger in the house. It made her nervous. And hospice only came three times a week."

"I'm sorry, man. You should have said something. We all would have helped more." Derek cleared his throat as Jake shook his head.

"It's all right. She was embarrassed and I was here. I just did what had to be done."

Chance blew his nose and threw the snot-filled tissue so that it landed on Jake's chest. "Well, she's right about one thing. You are glued to this ranch like stink on shit. You're just like her."

"I know." Jake looked him in the eye. "I can't help it. I drive into the city and I can't breathe. Too much noise. Too many people. I hate it."

Derek was the first one up. "I don't know about you guys, but I need a drink."

Jake actually smiled, and it felt good. Having his brothers here with him for this emotional roller coaster was good. "Whiskey's above the fridge."

They knocked back a couple shots in honor of their mother and got back to work. But instead of feeling invaded, Jake was relieved to let his mom's stuff go. It freed him in some indefinable way that he had no hope of understanding.

An hour later, the room was bare except for furniture, and they made quick work of hauling boxes out to his truck so he could drop them off at the nearest collection site.

"Now, let's get the furniture." Derek looked at Jake for confirmation and Jake nodded. It was time to move out of his boyhood room and into the master suite. Claire was right about that, too. Time to grow up. It didn't matter whether he liked it or not. This was his life and his house now, and he wasn't going to stay in his teenage bedroom for the next fifty years.

They took apart his mom's furniture and loaded most of it into one of his hay trailers. They moved the bed frame and dresser into his old room so he would have a bedroom for guests who needed a place to crash. The rest was going to town.

They gathered around the kitchen table, drinking whiskey and ice water when they were done and Jake had never been so glad for the company.

"What about the dishes and stuff?" Mitchell leaned back in his chair and tipped his glass toward the china hutch in the next room.

"You guys want any of it?"

"Naw. I took what I wanted when we split Mom's stuff at Christmas." Derek ran his hand over his head.

"Me, too." Chance leaned back until his chair was balancing on the back two legs. Mitchell tried to kick it out from under him, but Chance was too fast for him.

"Too slow, old man." Chance grinned, his light brown hair had grown longer since he'd quit the law firm, and he looked less haggard. There was a deep spark of happiness in his eyes that Jake had never seen before.

"Erin looks good on you, brother. You're all glowing and shit." Derek smirked at Chance from across the table.

"You know it. She's magical." Chance sighed, and the contented sound just rubbed Jake's nose in his own miserable existence. "You guys should see it. She has this set of wings—"

"Jesus, Chance. Shut the fuck up and have mercy on the mere mortals at the table." Mitchell chuckled and Chance smiled.

"She owns me. What can I say?" Chance looked over at Jake and his smile faded. "But you, little brother, look like someone just killed your dog. What the fuck has been going on with Claire since I left?"

When Jake remained silent, Chance looked to his right, to Derek, but it was Mitchell who answered.

"Claire Miller came back into town, fucked our boy's brains out, then dumped his ass...*again*."

"What?" Chance looked shell-shocked, which was how Jake felt. But still, he couldn't let his brothers badmouth Claire like that. It wasn't her fault.

"It was my fault, Chance. I was stupid. Don't talk shit about Claire."

"Screw that. I can't believe you, man. What were you thinking?" Chance reached over and smacked Jake on the shoulder, hard. "Stop thinking with your dick, Jake."

Jake shot to his feet, pissed. "Fuck you, Chance. Let's talk about Erin, shall we? About how she leads you around by the ball sac? How you quit your job to follow her around like a lovesick puppy? Or how you left us all behind as fast as you could? She must give one hell of a blowjob, asshole."

Chance went for Jake, grabbing him by the shirt and shoving him backward toward the living room. Which was just what Jake wanted. He was hurting and pissed, and hungry for a fight.

"Fucking A, Derek. I blame you for this." Mitchell shot up with Derek right behind him. Mitchell grabbed Jake from behind, wrapping him up in a bear hug as Derek did the same thing to Chance, trying to pull them apart.

"Chance, knock it off." Derek bellowed at them all and Jake froze, feeling like even more of a loser for taunting his closest brother that way.

He shrugged Mitchell off. "I'm fine. Let go."

Chance's eyes were spitting mad, but he wasn't fighting Derek's hold on him. "What the hell, Jake?"

"I'm sorry. Okay? Just don't talk shit about Claire. She's off limits." Jake turned and threw the front door open on his way to the barn. He'd take Widowmaker out for a nice long ride and clear his head. Today was testing every single one of his limits. Cleaning out his mom's stuff, starting the new bookkeeper, all the damn crying over his mother's card, and still no word from Claire.

Damn it to hell. He sent her another text.

Claire, please. I just want to talk.

He saddled Widowmaker and Chance came out of the house and joined him. Chance grabbed a saddle and went to work on Starlight, getting the mare ready to ride. "Mind if I join you?"

"No." Jake tightened the stirrup on the stallion's side and looked over the horse's back at his brother. "I'm sorry, Chance. I was out of bounds talking about Erin like that. I'm glad you're happy."

"No problem."

And that fast, they put it behind them. No drama. No bullshit.

When Chance was ready, they led the horses out of the stable and climbed on as Jake watched his truck and trailer pull out of the drive with Derek at the wheel and Mitchell riding shotgun.

"Where do they think they're

going?"

"They're dropping off Mom's stuff. Figured you have enough on your plate."

Jake's breath escaped him in a rush and he swallowed back another lump in his throat. He was done crying for the day. Fuck that shit; but taking his mom's things to the charity collection site had not been something he was looking forward to. "And you stayed behind?"

"To kick your ass."

Jake actually grinned. "You know that mare is ten years older, and slow."

"But I know the shortcut to Claire's house."

"What? No!"

But he was too late. Chance spurred the mare into action and he took off across the pasture toward the Millers' house.

Shit.

<><><>

Claire and Emily paced the edges of the large hotel's conference room in Washington, D.C., and listened to the excited conversation flowing around her. The assembled team was made up of archeologists and graduate students from all over the world. And at the head of the table sat a formidable Italian gentleman who had flown over from Naples to oversee the arrangements himself.

Mr. Fariello had detailed maps of the proposed dig sites, timetables for excavation and lists of the type and number of artifacts they were expected to find. A number of American museums were funding the dig, in exchange for borrowing a select number of items to put on display in a traveling exhibit.

"Miss Miller, Miss Davis, I am happy David recommended you both for the team. We had planned on going with another crew until he contacted me. Denver is very interested in hosting the exhibit next year. David assured me that you two could make that happen."

Claire turned on her heel to find Mr. Fariello at her shoulder. "Thank you. But I'm sorry. I don't know a David." She had no idea who this David might be.

Emily smiled, but shrugged. "We're flattered, but I don't know who he is either."

"David Levinson. He is an old friend from our days at Yale."

Holy shit. Dr. Levinson, from the museum in Denver? "Dr. Levinson?"

"Sí. Yes. Doctor. He did spend too much time with his nose buried in his books. But don't tell him I said so." Mr. Fariello held out his hand and Claire shook it first, followed by Emily.

"Thank you, I won't say a word." They were going to Italy! She could hardly contain her excitement, but for the first time her happiness was clouded by sadness as her phone buzzed in her jacket pocket. Again. Jake. He wouldn't stop. Which meant she couldn't stop thinking about him, not for five freaking minutes.

"Excellent. Tell David I'll send you home with some magnificent pieces for his exhibit." Mr. Fariello released her hand and wandered around the room greeting and shaking hands with the rest of the dig team. There were seven museums represented, three of them American. Denver, Chicago, and the

Smithsonian. Big players.

Guess she was taking the job in Denver after all.

Not that it mattered now. She and Jake were over. Done. Denver? California? Hell, she could move to Mars. It didn't matter. Not anymore.

Emily clapped her hands together. "I can't believe it! We're going to Italy! You're a goddess, Claire. Seriously. I don't know how you make so many miracles happen, but you do it every single time. Italy!"

"Italy." Claire smiled and hugged her best friend. The meeting was over and people were trickling out the door. She needed to get out of there and turn off her phone before Jake made her throw something. "We should go."

"Yes, please. I'm dead on my feet. I was still jet-lagged from Brazil when you called, but I wasn't missing this." Emily yawned and Claire felt sorry for her.

"Let get back to the hotel. You can order room service and crash."

"Perfect."

Claire walked to the table and found the rolling, black, executive chair where she'd left her leather laptop case open on the seat. She shuffled through the documents on the table where she'd been sitting for the last two days and sorted out the travel documents from the rest of the dig information. She had hours of reading and study ahead of her. And she needed to call Dr. Levinson to both thank him and officially accept the job. Emily had just been offered a job in Chicago, so both of them had to relocate. Luckily, she'd get to hang out with Emily on the dig. And, if this museum partnership worked out, there would be more excavations and more exhibits. She and Emily would travel the world together, just like they'd planned.

Levinson was one sneaky old man. She grinned as she thought of the nerdy museum director in his dungy little basement office. He knew the thrill of the chase, and he'd made that magic happen for her. She'd get to do what she loved and be the one to clean up the artifacts to get them ready for display. Win-win.

And when this job was over, she'd just have to hit him up for the next one.

And the next. He obviously had some pull with the museum board and could get them to fund projects. Luckily for her, the museum switched out at least one exhibit every three to six months, so she'd be busy.

It was perfect. Her life would be perfect, if not for the great big gaping hole in her heart with Jake's name on it. And living so close to him was just going to make it worse.

Her phone buzzed again and Claire pulled it out to check her messages.

Twenty-three texts and four missed calls, all from Jake. She ignored her voice mail, choosing instead to scroll through the texts quickly, seeing a lot of *I'm sorry, Call me, I just want to talk* and *Please answer.*

Not likely. She had a plane to catch tomorrow morning. And then she'd have to pack up, get to California, and sub-let her apartment. Then she had to find a place to live in Denver, pack up her stuff, and hire movers. The list made her tired just thinking about it.

Her mom would be happy that she was moving home. There was that, at least. And when Widowmaker threw her dad into a ditch again, she'd be close enough to help out without taking time off work. So, there were some good things.

Being closer to Jake wasn't one of them. That was officially going on her list of extreme torture. She had no idea how she was going to sleep at night, knowing he was just a half an hour's drive away.

She paused, frowning when she scrolled to the latest batch of texts from Jake.

Claire, I'm sorry. You don't have to answer me. I just wanted you to know you were right. I hired a bookkeeper. And my brothers came over. We packed up Mom's stuff. It was hard, but it's all gone.

Two minutes later, *I still don't know how to cook, but we can learn together...naked.*

Five minutes, *I miss you. Please come home.*

Ten minutes after that, *I love you with every cell in my body. You're my everything, Claire. Always.*

Shit. Claire shoved her phone in her bag and swallowed down the giant lump in her throat. How dare he do this to her now? How dare he tell her he loves her twice in the last three days when he'd never said it before? Why now, when nothing had really changed? Jake still wanted what he wanted, and she still couldn't give it to him.

He was tearing her in two.

Claire pasted a smile on her face and returned her attention to the present, back to the room full of archeologists and museum officials. Jake Walker was a heartache to deal with later.

Claire and Emily shook hands all around and said their goodbyes. As soon as they reached her rental car, she pulled out her cell phone and dialed Dr. Levinson's number.

He answered on the second ring.
"Hello?"
"Hello, Dr. Levinson. It's Claire Miller."
"Ah, yes. Miss Miller. Excellent to hear from you. How goes the meeting in D.C.?" She could hear the glee in his voice from two thousand miles away.

Well, that put her very last doubt to rest. "I think I owe you one, Doctor. Somehow the proposal I submitted to your board a few months ago has been unexpectedly funded. Miss Davis and I have both been invited to a dig in Italy in March."

"Ah, excellent. I guess you will officially need a job here at the museum, assuming you would like to accept their offer."

Time to put on her big girl panties and deal. "Yes. I'd be happy to accept your generous offer."

"Very well, Miss Miller. Welcome aboard. Human resources will be in touch and I shall expect to see you in my office in a few weeks."

"Thank you. I'll be there." Claire disconnected and stared at her phone. She had a little over a month to get her life together before she started her new job. She'd have to give notice at the University, too, and tell her friends out there goodbye. Nothing she hadn't done a half dozen times over the last few years, but this time, some of the sparkle was gone. This time, her joy was bittersweet, and she knew the reason.

Jake.

She opened her texting app and decided she'd better answer him.

I'll be back tomorrow. Talk to you then.

She had no idea what he wanted, and no idea what there could possibly be to say, but she owed him that much.

She hit send on the text and then called her parents' land line, the one place she could call and always count on them to be happy for her, no matter what.

Her dad answered, huffing and puffing. "Hello? Claire?"

"You're breathing like you just ran a marathon, Dad. Must be killing the broken ribs."

"I'm fine."

"You didn't take any pain meds today, did you?"

"Don't need 'em." Claire rolled her eyes. Totally called it. Her dad continued, "What's going on out there in our nation's capital?"

"Well, looks like I'm going to Italy."

"Good for you. Go get 'em. I knew you'd do great out there."

"Thanks, Dad." She heard her mom's mumbling in the background and her dad passed along the news.

"When are you going?"

"A couple months. It's a six-week excavation. We'll catalog our finds and go back again about six months later." Claire took a deep breath. Once she told her parents, there was no going back. "And I'm taking the job in Denver. Doctor Levinson pulled some strings. The Denver board is partially funding the dig."

"You're taking the job here, moving home?"

"Yep."

Her mom whooped in the background and Claire grinned through unexpected tears.

"We'll pick you up at the airport tomorrow, honey."

For better or worse, she was going home.

And it changed nothing between her and Jake. Nothing at all.

Chapter Sixteen

Jake and Chance galloped into the Millers' driveway at the exact same time, their horses' sides heaving and their cheeks bright red from the cold. The loud pounding of the horses' hooves drew the Millers from inside and their front door opened to reveal Mrs. Miller with a housecoat on, and Mr. Miller walking along behind her.

"Hi, boys!"

Chance walked Starlight closer to the porch and Jake followed. No sense being rude. He just hoped his stupid brother would keep his mouth shut.

No such luck.

"Hi, Mrs. Miller. We came to see Claire."

Mr. Miller came down the three steps leading to his front porch and walked over to Widowmaker with his arm hanging in a sling at his side. He smiled and patted the horse on the side of the neck as the stallion leaned down to greet the old man with a bump on the shoulder. True to form, Mr. Miller was a horseman, and he didn't hold a grudge against the horse, or blame the stallion for getting spooked. "She's not here, fellas. She's out in Washington, D.C., meeting with some bigwig from Italy."

"Italy?" Jake felt his stomach drop into his boots. She wasn't just leaving him, she was six-thousand miles away leaving him.

"Yep. Got a new dig starting soon. Six weeks in Italy digging up dead stuff." Mr. Miller rubbed Widowmaker's nose and fed the horse a carrot that he'd been hiding in his front pocket. "She's pretty excited about it, isn't she, boy?"

Widowmaker sniffed and snorted at Mr. Miller while Jake sat in stunned silence on the horse's back. Six weeks? She was going to Italy for forty-two days? The thought made his heart hurt almost as much as his head.

Chance filled in the awkward silence. "That's great news. We just thought we'd give these guys some exercise, and thought you might like to say hello."

"Good, good." Mr. Miller gave a final pat to his favorite horse's head and made his way back up the stairs to lean on the porch railing. "You boys better head back. It's getting dark out here. I'll let Claire know you stopped by."

Chance thanked them and turned Starlight around to head back to the ranch. Jake followed him half dazed, letting Widowmaker go where he wanted. Claire was in Washington, D.C., right now, meeting with some Italian bureaucrat who was going to send her to Italy for six weeks.

He could practically feel her slipping through his fingers like a ghost. The harder he tried to hold on, the faster she ran.

They let the horses cool down on a slow walk next to one another.

"So, what's the problem with Claire?"

Jake adjusted in his seat and rotated his head around on his neck to work some of the kinks out. "Hell if I know. I guess she's going to Italy."

"So? What difference does that make?"

"Can't exactly have a relationship with a woman who's in another country."

"That's just stupid. You're being a dumb ass."

"Excuse me?" Jake turned in the saddle to look at his brother.

"I said, that's stupid. People do it all the time."

Jake was working up an argument, but Chance kept right on talking.

"Look, when you guys ambushed me in my office about Erin, I was being a dumb ass. So, I know what I'm talking about. And trust me, you're being a dumb ass about Claire."

"She wants to leave. That's all I know. And I can't make her stay."

"No, you can't. But you *can* be the one she comes home to." Chance pulled up on Starlight's reins and Jake followed suit as Chance turned in the saddle to face him head-on. "Look, Jake. Here's the deal. Claire's smart and ambitious, and she wants to do something with her life. She's a lot like Erin. You can either get in her way, or you can accept it and adapt."

"I don't know how. She said she can't be happy on the ranch. She told me that I'm not enough for her. What the fuck am I supposed to do about that?"

Chance swung the end of his reins around to sting Jake's thigh. "You're even more stubborn than I was. Jesus. I'm starting to feel sorry for Claire. No wonder she left." Chance kicked Starlight in the side and the horse took off at a trot. Jake nudged Widowmaker to follow.

He didn't try to talk to his brother again until they were leading the horses into the barn to rub them down. "What do you suggest, brother? Because I'm all fucking ears here."

Chance pulled the saddle off Starlight's back and walked it over to the saddle horse at the end of the barn. When he had the saddle situated, he headed back to the horse to finish rubbing her down. "It's simple, Jake. Do you want Claire in your life, or not?"

"Yes."

"Then tell her, you idiot. And then, when it's time for her to go to on a wild adventure to Italy, or fucking

Antarctica, let her go."

"I don't understand."

Chance threw a brush at him. "I thought you were my smart brother."

"My dick is smarter than you."

"That being true, let me ask your dick this question. If you could have Claire for eleven months out of the year, would you want her?"

"Yes."

"Ten?"

"Yes."

"Nine? Seven? Five? At what magical, mystical number does that answer change?"

Fuck. He'd begged for three weeks with her. "It doesn't. I'm an idiot."

"Dumb ass. That's what I've been trying to tell you."

"What do I do now?"

"Marry her, before someone with more than shit for brains figures out how amazing she is. And when it's time for her to go, let her go. She'll come home to you. If she loves you, she'll always come home."

Feeling much more optimistic about the future, Jake pulled Widowmaker's saddle down and decided it was time to stir up some trouble.

"So, Mitchell's getting his balls kicked by a smoking-hot reporter he met down at the hospital...and she's a ginger." Mitchell was well known among the brothers for his life-long devotion to women with red hair.

"Oh, shit." Chance chuckled and shook his head. "That's classic. Tell me everything."

<><><>

Claire pulled her carryon down form the overhead bin and made her way up the narrow aisle of the commercial jet. The four-hour flight had taken its toll and she had spent most of it staring blindly at the notes she'd taken on the Italy project. She doubted she'd read five words—all she could think about was Jake.

He'd stopped texting her sometime yesterday afternoon. And, as much as the near-constant buzzing in her pocket annoyed her, the current silence made her feel even worse. She'd typed no less than a dozen messages to him. Everything from *I love you*, to *Please stop texting me*, but she hadn't sent a single one. Nothing felt right. Nothing was going to get her what she wanted.

With a sigh, she stacked her shoulder bag on top of her small suitcase and pulled them along to the train that would take her to the main terminal. Her mom was supposed to meet her there, at the top of the escalators on the baggage claim level. She rode the train in silence, avoiding looking at all the couples and families around her. They made her think about Jake, and cute little blond babies with blue eyes, fat fingers, and chubby cheeks.

God, some days she really hated being a woman. Why did she have to choose one life or the other? It sucked. Why couldn't she have a career and a man? Men did it all the time. They traveled and explored, and climbed fucking Mount Everest while the little woman waited at home for her conquering hero to return.

But a woman? No. She had to choose. Motherhood or career. Marriage or career. And if she had a job she hated, the choice would be easy. But she didn't. She loved her job and didn't want to give it up.

Maybe someday she could fall in love with a man who understood her. Maybe, somewhere out there in the world, there was a man strong enough to love her just the way she was — a man who wouldn't ask her to sacrifice everything she'd worked for. A man who could love her, without asking her to change.

But she didn't want someday. She wanted Jake.

The train stopped moving and the doors slid open. Claire followed the crowd up the double escalators to the main level of the terminal where the bright Colorado sunlight filtered into the large space through the tented ceiling. She got off the escalator and followed the stream of people toward Terminal East, where her mother was supposed to be waiting for her.

A large group of people had stopped moving ahead of her, and Claire weaved her way around them wondering what the heck was causing the traffic jam. The people seemed to be lingering, waiting to see what was going to happen.

Curious, she looked around to find what they were all waiting for and noticed two young women walking in front of a tall cowboy.

"If she says no, call me, cowboy." One of the women tilted her hips at the man as she walked by and Claire frowned. What the hell was that all about? And why were all these people standing around gawking?

"Excuse me." She turned sideways and wove her way through the small crowd, keeping her head down so she wouldn't trip over the people blocking the walkway. A single pair of boots stood in her way. She sidestepped, but they moved with her.

Frustrated, Claire looked up into a pair of oh-too-familiar blue eyes.

"Jake? What are you—" Her eyes dropped to a large white sign he was holding in front of his chest.

Claire, will you marry me? Was painted on it in bright red letters.

Confusion made her blink. What? Was this a joke? She turned her head left and right to find a sea of strangers' faces watching her with rapt attention.

She turned back to discover that Jake had dropped down on one knee and taken off his cowboy hat to set it on the floor. Someone catcalled from the upper balcony around the terminal. They were drawing a crowd, but Jake wasn't looking at any of them, he was staring up at her. He folded the sign in half and dropped it on the floor next to him. Claire looked down at him and held on to her suitcase for dear life. Without it, she was afraid she'd fall over. This couldn't be real.

When she looked into Jake's eyes, her Jake, she saw all the love she could have ever imagined. An old woman yelled out from somewhere in the back of the crowd. "Say yes, honey!"

Claire smiled but ignored everyone but the man she loved.

"Claire, I've been an idiot. I let you go once, but I'm not going to make the same mistake again. I love you. I've always loved you. I don't care how many trips you go on, or how long you're gone, as long as you always come home to me. Please, give me a chance. Forever, Claire. I don't want three weeks. I want forever." Her reached into his jacket pocket and pulled out the little black box she'd found in his drawer just three days ago. His hands were shaking as he opened it and pulled out the ring he'd bought for her so many years ago. "I've been waiting seven years to ask you this question, Claire. Marry me?"

Joy burst inside her and she nodded, tears gathering in her eyes. "Yes. I love you, Jake Walker. I've always loved you."

Jake slipped the ring on her finger as the crowd erupted in cheers. Claire ignored them all as Jake rose up and wrapped his arms around her, claiming her mouth in a kiss that rocked her to the core. This was real. This was Jake. This was forever.

Epilogue

One Week Later

Jake waited impatiently for his bride to reach him. Claire wore a stunning white sheath dress draped in the back with layers of smooth satin. It was simple, and elegant, and so very Claire. Her hair was up and her shoulders were bare and ready to be kissed. She held a bouquet of Lady Tresses; the white orchids were Claire's idea as a way to honor his mother.

The tiny Saint Malo Chapel was just a few miles from where they had grown up. The famous old chapel was built on a stone and overlooked one of the most stunning mountain vistas in all of Colorado. The Chapel on the Rock was truly beautiful, and he knew Claire loved this place as much as he did.

The church was only had six

wooden pews on each side, and those were less than half full. On both sides of the tiny sanctuary three long narrow windows curved at the top, letting in the bright Colorado sunlight. Overhead, bright red wood arched up in sharp geometric angles that held up the roof. The floor was stone everywhere but at the altar, where a bright red stretch of carpet covered the front quarter of the room.

The chapel usually only allowed Catholic weddings, but Mrs. Walker had been friends with Father John for over thirty years. He'd had dinner at the ranch once a month for as long as Jake could remember. Father John knew the Millers, and the Walkers, and every other family in the valley. He was practically family; and when Jake and Claire had gone begging, the priest had winked at them and given him the key. Told Jake to have it back to him before Sunday Mass.

As Claire got closer, her smile lit up her eyes and lifted the last of the dark shadows from his heart. This was where Jake had imagined marrying her. When they were ten, they'd ridden their horses here, snuck inside, and spent an afternoon exploring the rocks and valley. They'd been sitting in the front row as sunlight filtered through the windows and lit up Claire's young face and hair like an angel's halo. He'd thought she was the most beautiful girl he'd ever seen.

Hell, he still thought that. And now she was finally going to be his.

All three of his brothers were here, and Mr. and Mrs. Klasky. His head trainer, Mindy, and several of the guys that worked with him at the ranch were hanging around with big grins on their faces. Mrs. Gregory, his new bookkeeper, had straightened out his office in less than a week and now sat next to Mindy grinning from ear to ear. Claire's father was walking her down the aisle, without his sling, which Mitchell had already grumbled about. Mrs. Miller was beaming next to the Klaskys, and Claire's best friend, Emily, was standing opposite him serving as Claire's Maid of Honor. Every woman in the church was already wiping away tears.

Jake felt like he was about to

explode with happiness, and they were all crying.

Women.

Erin had even taken a day off from touring to fly in and attend the event. She sat in the front pew staring at Chance with a smile as bright as Claire's, the smile of a woman in love.

As Claire got closer, Chance leaned over and whispered in his ear. "For a dumb ass, you didn't waste any time."

"I wasted seven years. That was long enough."

Erin grinned from the front pew. "I think it's romantic."

Chance took one step, leaned over and kissed her. "You're such a girl."

Derek, Mitchell, and Chance stood at his side as he made Claire his wife and finally kept the promise he'd made to his mother all those years ago, the promise he'd made to himself. When the sunlight streaming through the window cast a beam of golden light in Claire's hair, he knew his mom was watching over them from heaven, just like she'd promised.

Marry Claire Miller and love her forever?

Check, Mom.
Check.

<><><>

Dear reader, thank you for spending time with Jake and Claire and the Walker Brothers. If you enjoyed this book, please take a moment to leave a review at your favorite retailer.

Jake and Claire's love song, Alone With You (by Lauren Kayley) coming soon to Apple iTunes & Amazon Music.

Read on for a sneak peek of Mitchell Walker's love story....

Up All Night
Love You Like A Love Song, Book 3
March 2016

Once upon a time Mitchell Walker fell in love...and trusted the wrong woman. That one mistake nearly cost him his future. His older brother, Derek, stepped in to take the fall. Mitchell has never forgiven himself for that day, and vowed to never trust another woman.

Now he is a young, successful surgeon. Women throw themselves at his feet, and he gives them what they want, as long as they don't ask for his heart. The strategy is working well for him until he meets freelance reporter Jessica Finley.

She's smart, she makes him laugh, and she sees right through his playboy persona. When Mitchell finds out she has links to the past he's tried so hard to forget, his life implodes, and Jessica is at the center of the detonation.

Jessica's fire may burn hot enough to keep him up all night, but will her love be strong enough to burn away the ghosts of his past and melt the ice around his heart?

Books by Michele Callahan

Love You Like A Love Song Series
Crash and Burn
Alone With You
Up All Night (March 2016)
Make Me Forget (April 2016)
Feels Like Forever (June 2016)

The Ozera Wars: Erotic Sci-Fi Space Opera
Rogue's Destiny
Queen's Destiny
Warrior's Destiny

Science Fiction/ Writing as M.L. Callahan
Alliance
Ryu's Paradox (A short story)
Defiance (coming soon)

The Timewalkers – Spring/Summer 2016
Red Night
Silver Storm
Blue Abyss
Black Gate
White Fire

Connect With Michele:
Facebook: michelecallahan.142
Twitter: @mlcallahan
Goodreads: Michele Callahan
www.michelecallahan.com

Song Lyrics: Alone With You

Copyright 2016, Michele Callahan and Lauren Kayley -- All Rights Reserved

*Jake and Claire's love song
coming soon to
Apple iTunes & Amazon Music*

When your arms are around me
When you kiss my lips
You take me over and
I lose myself in bliss
Storm I can't resist

<><><>
When I'm alone with you
Don't touch me baby
The world fades away
I forget the tears I cried
When I'm alone with you

<><><>
Why can't I just say no
I know this won't last
Drowning in forever
Tears us both in two

<><><>
Call me, talk to me

Tell me the truth
Am I too late
Was this fate
Or my mistake

<><><>

When I'm alone with you
Don't touch me baby
The world fades away
I forget the tears I cried
When I'm alone with you

Alone With You by Lauren Kayley coming soon to Apple iTunes & Amazon Music. Find out more at www.mlcallahan.com/music

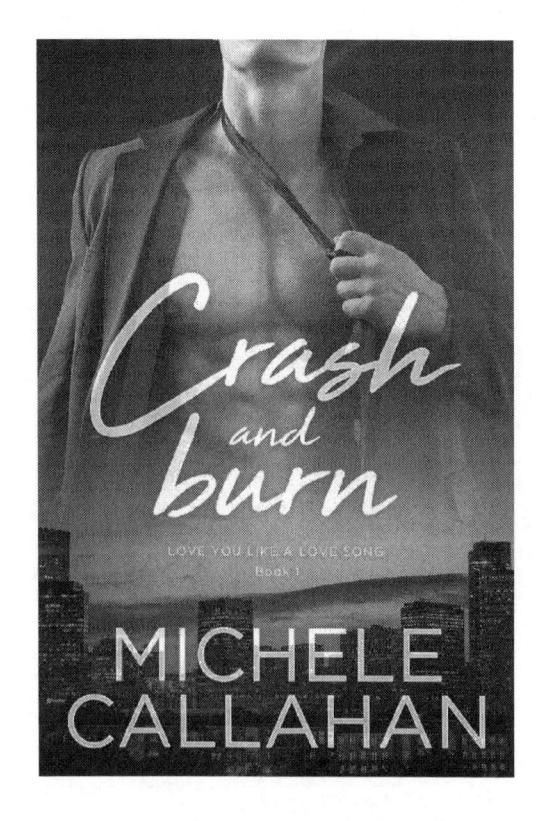

Crash and Burn
Love You Like A Love Song, Book 1

A childhood promise has Chance Walker picking up a guitar once again. Sure, he's been busy growing up, finishing college, and even law school. He made a promise to his dying mother and he's determined to keep it. While his guitar playing dreams were big when he was a kid, his skill is rusty and he hires Erin Michaelson to bring music back into his life. Not only is she incredibly talented, she's one of the sexiest women he's ever met. It's hard to focus on correct finger position when her sweet scent threatens to drive him out of his mind.

Less than twenty-four hours after his first lesson he sees her again, but this time she's on stage using another name and seducing an entire audience of men. He played the gentleman card once, and it got him nowhere. This time, all bets are off and he'll do whatever it takes to keep her. A single, sizzling backstage kiss will change both of their lives forever, because Chance soon realizes that Erin is not just an itch, she's an obsession that he refuses to live without.

Erin Michaelson spends her days teaching guitar and her nights on stage as her sexy alter-ego, Eva James. Music is her dream, her passion. All she wants is to say goodbye to a lifetime of scraping by, working two jobs, and paying for past mistakes. When a major record label exec hears her band play, she gets her big break. But life can be a real bitch, and meeting Chance now is just bad timing.

Problem #1: The record label wants her to dump her band and move to L.A. Problem #2: She hadn't counted on Chance Walker and the scorching heat of that first kiss. And last but not least is Problem #3: Is Chance really falling in love with the dull guitar teacher, or is he really just lusting after the sexy Eva James?

Will success make all of Erin's dreams come true? Or will falling in love make them both crash and burn?

Michele Callahan

Made in the USA
San Bernardino, CA
17 April 2016